# Anna's
# Hope

*Birdie L. Etchison*

*Heartsong Presents*

*To my friends on the peninsula, who love it as I do,
and especially to Jeanie Dunham who is an endless
source of information and help.*

**A note from the Author:**
*I love to hear from my readers! You may write to me at
the following address:*    **Birdie L. Etchison**
                            **Author Relations**
                            **P.O. Box 719**
                            **Uhrichsville, OH 44683**

**ISBN 1-57748-249-2**

**ANNA'S HOPE**

*Cover illustration by Peter Pagano.*

PRINTED IN THE U.S.A.

## one

The *T.J. Potter*, loaded with passengers, cows, dogs, chickens, and assorted baggage, swooshed its way down the Columbia River. Most people were headed for Astoria and parts south. A few would ferry across the Columbia to Megler Landing on the Washington side.

It was to this place that Anna Galloway had promised to go. A nurse was needed to help the only doctor in the primitive area. Anna's older brother, Albert, had been most persuasive in talking her into leaving the comforts of Portland, her home with her younger brother Ben, and all the other family and friends she'd just met in the two weeks since coming from Iowa.

After graduating from nursing school in Iowa City, Anna had worked at a hospital in Cedar Rapids. There she received word that her mother, Sarah, was dying. Could she come west to Oregon?

The time for a change could not have been more perfect. Joseph, the man she loved, had decided they could not marry. "You were meant to be a nurse, Anna, but I need a wife."

Joseph's words still stung, and now Mama's death added to the ache deep inside her. Perhaps she did like nursing too much, but it was a calling and wasn't one supposed to listen to God's voice, the urging to be, to do?

The wind whipping off the river blew Anna's short curls—the few that stuck out from under the navy blue, wool cloche she clutched tightly to her head with one hand. It was midsummer of 1912 and Anna wondered how it could be so chilly in July.

"I've never seen such a cold summer wind," she cried to Albert. "In Iowa, the corn would be growing overnight, along with the tomatoes in Mama's garden. I'm beginning to wonder about going to this place surrounded by water. I'm a farm girl at heart. I like land. A place to put my feet."

Albert, dark and ruggedly handsome, smiled at Anna. She was just a year younger than he was, but she had always acted older, and had the upper hand.

"Yes, there is a heap of water." He fingered his short, well-clipped beard. "Soon we'll dock in Astoria. From there you'll take the ferry across the Columbia, then ride the railroad with its passengers and wide assortment of animals—whatever needs to be transported—west to the North Beach Peninsula."

"Once I get there, I'm staying put." Anna's chin jutted out with determination. She breathed deep gulps of air that nearly took her breath away. Whitecaps appeared, making her think of pictures she'd seen in books of the rolling waves of the Pacific Ocean. She never dreamed she'd someday see it, and now she was almost there.

Hills bordered both sides of the river, giving Anna some comfort. She pulled her long coat closer, her broad shoulders buffeting the wind. "At least there is *some* land."

"Of course, not much is inhabited by man."

"Oh!" Anna cried. Her voice seemed to be snatched by the wind and thrown to the depths of the river. She barely heard Albert's voice and had to shout into his ear or repeat her words. "Why did I ever let you talk me into this?" She tried to smile.

"Because you are needed. When Dr. Snow came to Astoria, asking for nurses, and nobody accepted the position, I thought of you. With five years' experience, you fit his request well."

"You haven't convinced me, Albert. All I wish is for this ride to be over."

Albert threw back his head and laughed the hearty, loud Galloway laugh. "Your journey is far from over, Anna." He chuckled again, then looked at his watch. "You'll probably arrive in Seaview by sundown."

Anna disliked it when Albert teased her. He had done so when they were children. That seemed so long ago now. Shortly after Anna had left for nurse's training at the University of Iowa, Albert had also left, looking for adventure in the Pacific Northwest. He'd never returned to Iowa and had no intention of ever doing so.

"How can it take so long?" Anna asked. She could have walked to the lower level where it was warmer, but it wouldn't have been nearly as interesting. Besides, she felt safer watching the waves, leaning in the direction the boat went. She marveled at how the river whipped up such monstrous waves, though she didn't want to admit it to her brother.

"It's farther west, that's why." He cleared his throat. "I'll be staying in Astoria, you know."

"What?" Anna turned and stared at Albert, but there was no laughter in the dark eyes now. "You mean you aren't going the rest of the way with me?"

He pointed across the river to where she saw the vague outlines of buildings suspended in the air. "That's the fish seining fields where I'll be working now. I don't live on the peninsula anymore."

"But. . . ," she sputtered. "Why didn't you tell me?"

Anna, fiercely independent, had been on her own the past several years now. She had a mind of her own—"a stubborn streak" Mama had called it. She liked trying new things, but this was different. This place was at the end of the world.

Albert touched her shoulder, then hugged her for a brief moment. "I just didn't fill in all the details, but you'll do fine here. The most important reason is that you are needed. Besides, I thought you were ready for adventure."

Thoughts of Joseph flashed through her mind again and she nodded. "Yes, I am wanting to do something new." How could she have forgotten?

"Excuse me," a voice said at her elbow. "I couldn't help overhearing." He offered a hand. "Peter Fielding. I'm on my way up past Seaview and can make sure you get off at the right place." His eyes met Anna's surprised gaze.

"You're going on the same train?"

Peter laughed. "There is only one way to get to the peninsula. We'll ferry across, then catch the Clamshell Railroad—"

"Clamshell railroad!" Anna declared. "Are the tracks made of clamshells?"

Both Albert and Peter laughed. Then, as if noting Anna's displeasure, Peter explained, "It's what the locals call it— the train that runs by the tide, and is never on time."

Anna raised her hand, wanting to add emphasis to her statement, and in that moment her hat flew off, sending her thick brown curls to dancing. She lunged for the hat, but Peter grabbed it. His dark, warm eyes seemed to mock her as he handed it over. Anna blushed deeply while putting it back on her head. "Thank you."

"You're certainly welcome." If he hadn't caught the hat when he had, it could have been over the railing and into the raging waters. It was the last gift from her mother, and she loved it dearly for that reason.

"We do need nurses," Peter said. "Doc Snow is overworked, and the only nurse we had left for California."

Anna found the young man disconcerting without knowing why. Words stayed inside her, a rarity in her case, since little ruffled her. She turned to Albert, hoping he'd carry on the conversation.

"Mr. Fielding, I'd like to take you up on your offer to see that Anna gets on the train and off at the Seaview Station. I understand there is a boardinghouse nearby."

Peter smiled. "A short distance, and she'll love the proprietor, Miss Bessie."

The *T.J. Potter* turned and headed toward the bank. Astoria. The small fishing town on the Oregon side. Anna knew it was one of the earliest settlements on the West Coast, and boasted the first post office. Fishing was the livelihood. Everywhere Anna looked there were boats and more boats. A few houses dotted the surrounding hills. Civilization. It looked inviting. Maybe she should stay here.

They pulled up to a dock with much bumping and clamoring about as people gathered their belongings. At last it stopped and Anna knew she'd feel land under her feet. Firm, steady land. It would seem good, even if it was only for a few minutes.

Albert jumped into action. "I'll get your baggage, Anna."

She'd brought one medium-sized trunk. It contained two nurse's uniforms, a cape, her cap, and four dresses; two were good, two for every day. Two pairs of shoes were in the bottom.

"I must get back to the seining fields," Albert ex-plained to Peter. "I'd meant to see Anna settled in, but I stayed in Portland longer than intended and am a day late as is. I'm the assistant manager of the operation."

"But, Albert, when will I see you?" A sudden fear washed over Anna.

"I'll catch the ferry over a week from Sunday. See how you're faring." He bent down, brushing a quick kiss on Anna's cheek. Before she could protest further, he tipped his hat and was off, going up the gangplank. She turned to find Peter Fielding watching her, waiting.

"Here. I'll handle the trunk. We'd better get in line."

"And where is your luggage? How will you manage mine also?"

"I have none."

"None?"

"I went to Portland yesterday on business and am now returning home."

"I see."

The ferry was loading and soon Anna was going from a large boat to a smaller one.

"Sometimes the *T.J. Potter* pulls up over at Megler Landing, but today there were people, like your brother, who needed to get off in Astoria, and passengers who needed to get on there."

Anna felt some bit of comfort in having Peter Fielding see to her needs, but she disliked being beholden to anyone. Yet there was something nice about him, especially the warmth in his eyes.

"It'll be a short trip across the river." Peter glanced at his pocket watch. "And I think the train will be ready and waiting."

"How far must I go on the train?" Trains Anna was used to. She'd taken the train on her ride out from Iowa. When Mama got sick, she could think of nothing but going to Oregon to see her one last time. Sarah had died a week later, and Anna was glad she'd come. Glad she'd left Iowa behind.

*I'll forget Joseph if it's the last thing I ever do,* she thought now. *Perhaps there is a life for me here.*

"Not too many miles. At least you're not going to the North End. We'll go past Chinook, Ilwaco, then Seaview. Just be glad you're not going to Nahcotta."

"Nahcotta?" *What strange names,* Anna thought. *Astoria, Nahcotta. Chinook, Ilwaco.*

"Indian names," Peter said then, as if reading her mind.

"Oh. Are there Indians, Mr. Fielding?"

"Of course. All civilized, to be sure."

"You're teasing me."

A smile played about his full mouth. "Maybe just a bit, but there are a few Indians living there. All friendly."

Before long the ferry arrived at Megler and the train was waiting. Anna held onto her hat, lifting her heavy coat and dress just enough so she could mount the steps. Soon they were settled into adjoining seats.

"I will see you to the boardinghouse," Peter said, "perhaps borrow a horse from Bessie, as my family is waiting."

"Tell me about your family," Anna said.

"I have two children."

*And a wife,* Anna almost said. She had a habit of finishing people's answers, but she'd stopped in time. Not that she cared that he was married. She wasn't coming here to find a husband, though her mother had worried about her, begging her to find someone, settle down, but that was Mama. She supposed all mothers felt that way about unmarried daughters, and Anna knew Sarah had prayed often for all her children, wanting them to be settled and happy.

"What ages are they?" Anna glanced up to see a pained expression in the brown eyes. "Oh. Did I say something wrong?"

"No. You'll get a chance to meet them. Catherine is seven, Henry five."

"I will certainly look forward to that," Anna said, wanting to ask about his wife.

The train continued chugging toward its destination as Anna stared out the window. The exhaustion she'd felt earlier had abated some.

"Children are a blessing," Anna said then. She watched the different shades of green on the hillside as the train passed. She'd never seen such immense trees or so many. The various shades of green fascinated her. This was nothing like Iowa, where everything was brown with a few trees scattered across the land.

The feeling of desolation hit again. She thought of her family back in Portland. Brother Ben, his wife Emily with baby Clifford and another baby on the way. And Pearl, now married. How could her baby sister marry before she did? At least Anna had Albert. He was the one responsible for her coming here, leaving her to the whims of another person as if he didn't care a bit.

*O God,* Anna prayed. *Help this to work. Help me to be of use to someone. Guide my steps.*

She thought of the Bible buried deep in her trunk. A verse came to mind now—one Sarah had repeated to her many times as she was growing up on the Iowa farm. "Be still and know that I am God" (Psalm 46:10).

"Anna," Mama used to say, "there is no way God can help you. You're never still long enough to hear Him."

*Yes, God, I've not been still much of my life, but something tells me I am going to be still—very still—from now on. For once I'm going to rely on You all the way.*

"You're smiling." Peter's voice broke through her thoughts.

Anna opened her eyes and found Peter Fielding's warm gaze on her. His look was expectant and her heart gave a sudden lurch.

" 'Be still and know that I am God,' " Anna repeated then. "It's a verse my mother used to read to me, and somehow it seems most fitting now. I'm not sure why I came, or if I'll like it, but I guess I'll find out soon."

"You came because we need you, Miss Anna. As for the liking it, I think you will once you get used to the rain and wind."

Anna sighed. "I wish I could be more sure." She tried to relax, as she straightened her skirt of black bombazine. "Tell me," she said then. "What is the hospital like? How many rooms?"

*"Hospital?"* Peter looked perplexed. "We have no hospital on the peninsula."

"No hospital?" A strange feeling overcame Anna. Hadn't Albert said there was a hospital? Or had he?

Perhaps she'd been so caught up in the adventure she hadn't even asked.

Anna finally found her voice. "I assumed there would be a hospital. How can I tend to patients if there is not?"

Peter shrugged. "Like Doc Snow does. You go to them."

"But how can I do that when I don't have a means of transportation or know where things are—"

"They'll give you a horse—"

"A horse!" Anna shrieked.

"Oh, no!" Peter hit his head with his palm. "Don't tell me you don't ride horses."

Anna just stared for a long moment. Of course she could ride a horse. She'd learned at an early age on the farm, but that had been eons ago.

"Do you want to go back to Portland?"

Anna considered that option, then shook her head. "I'm not a quitter, Mr. Fielding. I just wish I'd known ahead of time, that's all."

"Your brother may not have known."

Anna looked grim. "Oh, he knew all right. That's Albert for you."

She settled back against the seat, her mind whirling with thoughts. No hospital. No house where patients came. She'd be a traveling nurse. Riding on a horse, to places she knew nothing about. Well, Albert had been right about one thing: this area was far more primitive than anywhere Anna had ever lived. It would certainly be a challenge.

She closed her eyes and once more listened for God's voice, wanting to be reassured, but all she heard was the clickety-clack of the wheels as the train headed further west. West to her new home. West to fulfill her career, to nurse those who needed help. Would she see Peter Fielding again? She doubted it, but time would tell. She adjusted her hat and leaned farther back in the cushioned seat.

## two

By the time the small train chugged into yet another depot, darkness had crept throughout the car.

"We're here, Anna." Peter Fielding stood, offering his hand. "I'll get your trunk, then walk you to the boarding-house."

Anna straightened her dress and the hat and felt a tingle in her toes. She followed Peter down the aisle, and down the steps, taking the hand he offered her. She shivered from the sudden chill of the night. No stars shone overhead. It was dark. Black and eerie. But there was a sound, a roaring noise she could not identify. Could this be the ocean? She sniffed the air. It smelled different, too, and she decided it must be the salt in the atmosphere. She wished she could see the ocean waves. Sudden fear of the unknown hit again.

"O God," she whispered, "if this is where I'm supposed to be, please help me to know."

"Did you say something?" Peter asked, turning as he placed Anna's trunk on a small rail cart.

"Only a plea to my Father above," Anna said. She shivered again. It was a damp sort of cold that chilled a body to the bone immediately.

"We've just one block to go, then you'll have a place to sleep, and a spot of tea before you retire. You'll adore Bessie."

"A cup of tea would be delightful." Anna held her coat closer.

The house appeared. Shrouded in darkness, it looked immense.

Anna followed Peter up the steps onto a glassed-in sun porch.

He banged on the door. "I'm sure Bessie will have a room for you. She's come to expect travelers on the evening train."

The door sprang open and a large, buxom lady exclaimed, "Is that ye, Mr. Peter Fielding?"

Anna felt comfort from the voice, and her shoulders relaxed. She had an accent. She must be a Scot, just like Anna's nursing supervisor back in Iowa. She smiled and nodded.

"Brought you a guest, Miss Bessie—one who will be staying longer than a day or two."

"I wondered if the train might not bring some boarders to my home this night." She held out her arms, hugging the bedraggled Anna.

"I'm Bessie McGruder, head cook and owner of this place. Ye both come on in."

"This is Anna Galloway," Peter said. "She's the nurse Doc Snow's been expecting."

"Land a goshen, if he won't be happy to see ye."

"I was expected then?" Anna asked as she followed Peter and Bessie into the house. She hadn't been sure that he'd received her letter of acceptance.

"He did mention someone might come, but he's been disappointed before."

Anna tried to smile, but her face felt frozen, her body numb.

Bessie, as if reading Anna's mind, led her into the dining area. "Sit while I fix tea and a bowl of leftover soup.

Don't always have soup left, but the good Lord knew I'd be a needing some this night."

Anna nodded and sank against a thick bank of pillows in what looked to be a window seat in the combination dining-living room. Bessie turned to Peter. "And if ye'd be so good as to take that trunk up to the third floor—to the room at the far right, I'd be ever so grateful. I think this young lady would enjoy the view from there."

Anna heard the roaring sound, even inside the house, and wondered if she'd ever feel warm again. She wasn't sure how long she'd be staying at the boardinghouse, but a quiet peace came over her and she felt comforted by this woman who had thrown her arms around Anna when she didn't even know her. It was almost as if Mama had been there.

Though Anna hadn't been around Sarah in the past few years, she would always remember how her mother tended to her needs. Anna thought about the rainstorms that hit Iowa every spring with fair regularity. Everyone rushed out to pick as much corn as they could, filling the gunnysacks to overflowing. Anna's arms had ached, but she couldn't stop. They couldn't sell it now, but would use it as feed for the horses and cow. Anna remembered her mother lifting her sodden dress from her shoulders, and then pressing a cup of hot tea into her hands. The warmth of the cup, made her teeth finally stop chattering. . .

"I know how tiring that trip can be," Bessie was saying, bringing a tray in. "My son used to make it—" She turned away and a sudden stillness filled the room. "Not that God ain't a-takin' care of 'im, because I know the Almighty is. . ."

"Your son?" Anna asked, wanting to know more.

"He died. It was a fever that took 'im when he was twenty-five."

"Oh, I'm so sorry."

Bessie patted her hand. "Don't ye go a feelin' sorry for me. I have family plenty enough right here, don't I, Mr. Fielding?"

Peter had come back down and nodded. "Yes, Miss Bessie has plenty of folks she thinks of as family, and we all think she's right special."

"Are you having tea?" Bessie asked.

"No. I must return home. Fetch the children from my neighbor, Doris Yates. I'll take ole Ned, if you don't mind."

Bessie hugged Peter briefly. "Sure thing. Ye can bring Ned back whenever. And give those two of yours a hug for me."

Anna wanted to say the same, but didn't feel it proper. She bade Peter good night, thanking him again for all his help.

"Such a loss," Bessie said, once the door was closed. "I don't suppose he told you about Callie."

"Callie?"

"His wife."

"No. I wondered why he had to pick up his children—"

"Died, she did. About a year ago. Right after Dr. Snow came. Doc tried everything he could, but the good Lord took her, and only He knows the reasons. As it says in the Book, the rain falls on the just as well as the unjust."

Anna set her cup down harder than she meant to. "Seems we all have losses." She thought of Sarah again, but it was different. Sarah'd had a full life; Peter's wife had been young and had left two children.

Bessie stood. "Now as soon as ye are ready, I'll show ye your room. I think ye will like it. Just last summer I put up pink rosebud wallpaper."

Anna loved the room the minute she saw it. Since it was on the top floor, the ceiling was slanted, yet it was spacious and airy. She liked the square brass headboard, the colorful quilt, the multicolored braided rug. A small vanity was in one corner, a massive wardrobe filled the wall opposite the bed. A faint smell of lavender made her smile, remembering that fragrance from years ago when Sarah had made lavender sachets for Christmas.

"I see ye is clasping your hands." Bessie set the lamp on a small end table topped with a crocheted scarf. "That's always a good sign."

"It's beautiful," Anna said softly. "I will be content here."

The older woman beamed. "I hope the train's whistle won't bother ye, but it can't be helped. That's why I put ye on this side of the house, hoping it wouldn't be quite as loud."

"I will be so tired, nothing will waken me," Anna said. Suddenly all she could think of was sinking into the bed, pulling the thick quilts up under her chin, and closing her eyes.

*⁂*

It wasn't daylight that wakened Anna the next morning, nor was it the sound of the early morning train pulling into the Seaview station; it was the smell of bacon frying and biscuits baking that coaxed her from her sleep.

At first she didn't remember where she was, and then it all came back. This was her new home on the North Beach Peninsula, miles from brother Albert, and many,

many miles from Portland, where the rest of her family lived. She'd made the decision to come here, so she would make the best of it. The Galloways had never been quitters. She'd do her best to help the sick in this isolated spot. Just knowing she was needed gave her some small comfort.

She bounded to the window with its white, lace curtains and peeked out. Anna's breath caught in her throat at the beauty of the blue water with the frothy white waves. Mesmerized, she watched the waves rolling in, then rolling out, some more boisterous than others. The ocean stretched forever, as far as she could see, out beyond the blue horizon. She pulled herself away from the window. Enough lollygagging. There were things to do today. One of the first was to unpack, then iron her uniforms.

Anna chose a pale green muslin and tried to smooth the wrinkles out with her fingers. Wrinkles couldn't be helped, as she'd packed the trunk tight. Hurriedly, she ran a brush through her short hair, once again barely recognizing herself in the mirror. She'd chopped off most of her hair last week. It had been an impulsive moment and she wondered now if she might regret the decision.

Slowly, wondrously, Anna descended the stairs, taking note of the photographs, the artwork that lined the wall.

"Anna! And top of the mornin' to ye!" Bessie smiled at the boarders seated around the large, rectangular table. "This is Miss Anna Galloway, our new boarder and nurse!"

"Good morning," voices called out. Anna noticed all the boarders were older with the exception of one young woman. Anna nodded and smiled.

"I trust ye slept well?" Bessie asked.

"Like I haven't slept in a year," Anna replied, looking again at the faces around the table.

After introductions, Anna took a small helping of scrambled eggs, two strips of bacon, and one baking-powder biscuit.

"Ye can certainly eat more than that," Bessie said, looking down the long table at Anna.

"Mama said one can always go back for more," Anna explained, dabbing berry jam on her biscuit.

"And in a boardinghouse if you don't get it while the gettin's good, you might miss out," said Miss Fern on her right.

"That's only when Doc comes," Mr. Webster added. He touched his short, straggly beard. "He's the one with the appetite."

After breakfast, Bessie took Anna's plate and shooed her on up stairs. "I have kitchen help. They'll take care of this. Take this day to rest. Unpack. Walk to the beach—though—" She looked out the window. "I don't think the walking will be good—not with that fog rolling in."

Anna looked out the bay window and sighed with disappointment. A walk to the beach had been on her agenda for the morning. However there would be time for that later.

"When can I meet the doctor?" Anna asked then. She could be lazy one day—perhaps that would be permitted—but she longed to start work. She hadn't been nursing for three weeks now.

"Doc Snow comes for lunch, barreling through that door at 11:45 sharp. I can set my clock by him."

"There's plenty of time for unpacking—"

"And a tour of the house, if ye'd like."

Anna smiled. "I'd like that very much."

She followed Bessie up the winding staircase to the second floor, looking at the highly polished wood. She'd been too tired to notice last night and too hungry this morning.

"The captain bought this place before it was finished. The first owner died and his wife moved back to Portland."

"The captain?"

"That's what I call my husband. He was a captain when I met him and a captain when he died." Bessie's eyes looked up. "The good Lord gave us twenty wonderful years."

Anna wondered how many years Peter and Callie'd had.

"Captain fell in love with this place—said it reminded him of his boyhood home back in Scotland."

"Was this before you were married?"

Bessie shook her head. "I met him on the *T.J. Potter* coming down the river just like ye came yesterday."

Anna thought of Peter again. Had God sent her here to care for two motherless children, or to be a nurse? She chastised herself of even thinking such thoughts. Besides, she still had feelings for Joseph.

"We have five bedrooms on this floor and a sitting room. Some call it a reading and writing study," Bessie went on.

The room, painted a sunny yellow, had two small sofas and a table with a checkerboard waiting, as if hoping someone would choose to play a game. The window beckoned and she looked out once more at the pounding surf, surrounded now by the incoming fog.

"The wood is the finest Douglas fir ye'll ever lay eyes on. Hauled up the river by the builder. He was a Portland businessman, ye know."

"It's all so beautiful," Anna said. Each room had vivid colors, drapes at the windows, and small throw rugs.

"Is this the captain?" Anna asked, noting she'd seen the picture of the same man in all the rooms thus far. He had a gruff look and wore a seaman's cap.

Bessie nodded. "That's my captain all right. He was lost at sea; storm came up that fast!" Her face looked drawn. "Never seen anythin' like it."

Anna gazed at the view from one of the windows and wondered how anyone in his or her right mind would want to go out in that water to fish. The Columbia River had been rough, but this ocean looked far more treacherous and with the fog coming in, one could get off course easily.

The two women arrived at the top floor and Bessie promised to show her the rest later. "Ye tend to the unpacking—whatever ye must do. Come down when ye like."

Anna hung her dresses and uniforms in the wardrobe and placed her shoes on the floor, her mirror and brush on the vanity. The window beckoned again, and this time she could not see the waves crashing against the shore, because of the fog, but the sound had a lulling, magical quality. She got a chill. Used to hot weather, sunshine beaming from sunup to sundown, as all Iowa summers were, Anna knew this cool climate would take getting used to.

She placed her Bible on the desk and pulled out the small chair. Withdrawing a small tablet, she wrote a note to Emily and Ben.

*I have arrived in Seaview. It is so different from what I expected—so quaint. I'm staying at a huge boardinghouse. There is no hospital here. Imagine my dismay upon discovering that. The doctor needs a nurse, so perhaps I will be busy after all.*

*I know God shall take care of me and has brought me here for a purpose. I hope to go to work soon.*

*Emily, take care of yourself, and give Clifford a piggyback ride, Ben.*

*Love to Pearl and Paul. I hope someone will come to visit me soon. I miss all of you tremendously.*

*With warmest regards,*
*Anna Galloway*

Anna sealed the letter and took it with her as she descended the two flights of stairs. She saluted the photograph of the captain on the second floor landing, and noticed another man with a formal look. *President William McKinley*, the caption read. She remembered he had been assassinated in 1901, six years before her father died. She liked his strong chin, the bold, piercing eyes. He made her think of Papa.

A wonderful smell of beef stew and cornbread wafted in from the kitchen as Anna entered the main room. The table was set with blue willoware plates, cups, and thick, well-used pieces of flatware.

On cue, as the mantel clock gonged the quarter hour, the door opened and a tall, broad-shouldered figure came into the kitchen, filling it with his presence. "Is that beef stew I smell? Bessie, you're a darling."

His hand reached out to grab a chunk of cornbread, and Bessie playfully swatted him. "Oh, and be gone with ye!

Can't even wait until we've sat and asked the Lord's blessing?"

"The Lord knows I'm thankful for my food, especially when I come here, my dear Bessie—" He stopped, and Anna turned to find herself looking straight into the eyes of *the* Dr. Snow, the man she had come to work with. She trembled unexpectedly as their gazes met and held.

"You didn't tell me we had company."

"That's because I didn't know she was a coming until last night. Came up on the *T.J. Potter* and over on the train. Anna, this is Dr. Wesley Snow whom I've been speaking of. And Dr. Snow, this is Anna Galloway, all the way from Iowa State."

Anna stepped forward and held out her hand. His piercing gaze might have stopped one younger, but Anna had never been shy. "I trust you received my letter of recommendation?"

He towered over Anna, his square face showing surprise. Then he smiled as he took her hand. "Yes, I received it. My regret is there was not time to answer."

"I came on ahead, anyway," Anna said. "If you had no need for me, I planned on returning to Portland. I have family there." She wondered if she should mention she'd had second thoughts after the lengthy ride on the *T.J. Potter*. She decided not.

His eyes were intense, his face clean shaven. "You have a degree in nursing, I understand."

"Yes. I finished my schooling five years ago at the University of Iowa School of Nursing. Graduated with the class of 1907."

The eyes suddenly twinkled and Anna felt herself relax. "My dear woman, you can be of use here. Do not think otherwise. It's just that I did not know when to expect you—"

"That's because my mother was gravely ill," Anna interrupted, "and I could not leave her side. She passed on a week ago."

"I'm dreadfully sorry to hear that." His face went somber. "I just said to Miss Lizzie Myles, my housekeeper, that what this peninsula needs is a nurse—and here you are!"

Anna felt her cheeks redden under his steady gaze. "I had thought there would be a hospital here, but Mr. Fielding, the young man who assisted me last evening, said there was none."

"Yes and there should be, but we use the boardinghouse here, and I've turned my home into a hospital of sorts. I can do operations and treat patients there nicely now. The rest of the time I visit the sick and do what I can."

"I am ready to start work straightaway," Anna said.

"Good. Good. I have a maternity patient who doesn't want to leave the peninsula. I'm a mite concerned about her."

The dinner gong sounded. Soon Mr. Webster and Miss Fern came down the stairs, while Cora, the younger woman, sauntered in from the porch. The table wasn't crowded, but Bessie said to wait until the weekend when the *T.J. Potter* brought more people to the peninsula.

Dr. Snow removed his coat and sat at the opposite end of the table from Anna. Soon everyone was chattering. She listened while he told about the beached whale he'd seen the day before. "Of course, there's never a thing you can do but let it lie there and rot."

Anna made a face. It was hardly the topic for meal conversation.

"I certainly hope you don't have a squeamish stomach—"

Anna looked him straight in the eye. "No. I assure you I do not, but what of the others?"

He roared then as if she'd said something amusing. "They're not even listening to me."

Anna turned back to her stew, noticing that the good doctor had finished both his stew and two chunks of cornbread. His face lit up when Bessie brought bowls of chocolate pudding with mounds of whipped cream on top for dessert.

"Bessie, each meal is better than the last."

Anna decided to say no more and hurried to finish the stew. It was good, but it was hard to swallow past the hard knot in her throat. She'd come prepared to like the doctor, but he seemed brusque, almost flippant. Finishing the pudding in three bites, Dr. Snow pushed his chair back. "You'll do, Miss Galloway. You look quite capable."

Before Anna could respond, he had stridden to the doorway. "I must go, but if you'd like, you can come first thing in the morning to my makeshift hospital. Bessie can give you directions. You brought uniforms, I trust."

"Of course."

He looked at her strangely, then asked, "Do all the nurses wear their hair short in Iowa?"

Anna felt remorse for her action when she'd whacked off the long, brown hair. She had been more than blessed with the thick Galloway hair that had a mind of its own. Many times she'd lamented trying to pin it up to her supervisor's satisfaction.

With it shorn, it would be so much easier to wash and brush.

"Do you have a problem with my hair?" Anna asked with sudden boldness.

He shrugged. "I suppose not, but—"

Anna's face flamed for the second time since meeting the doctor. "I cut it right after my mother died, as she wouldn't have approved."

"Hair is a woman's crowning glory; says so in the Good Book."

"Yes, so it does." Anna didn't know what else to say.

"But—" Wesley Snow smiled. "I think short hair might be a good idea. It's why I shave my face each day." He fingered his smooth chin. "Hair carries germs, you know." He stood and held out his hand again. "I look forward to having you work with me. I'll expect you in the morning, around seven. Now I must get on to my next patient."

Anna had a sudden impulse to ask if she could go with him. It would only take minutes to don her uniform, though it was wrinkled. She found she didn't want to wait until morning, but as he turned and walked back through the kitchen, Anna knew it would be better to go with a cleanly pressed uniform. And her cap might hide the fact that her hair was short.

*Did Dr. Snow mean it,* she wondered later, *that short hair was a good idea, or was he just being kind?* But as Anna was soon to discover, Dr. Snow was never kind for the simple sake of being kind. Anna wondered about his brusque, abrupt manner, yet she liked how he looked you square in the eye, his gaze never wavering.

"An honest man always looks you in the eye," Papa

used to say. "If he cain't, don't trust him behind your back."

She stood at the parlor window listening to the surf and the sound of horses clip-clopping down the road.

Anna wondered again about Joseph, remembering that night when he'd broken her heart. "Anna, I will always remember you with fondness, but I love another. Besides, you have your nursing career ahead of you."

For a long while Anna had wondered what she would do without Joseph in her life, but looking back she realized she had done just fine, and would continue to do so. With fierce determination, she turned from the window and took her empty cup and saucer to the kitchen. Tomorrow was the beginning of a new and promising day.

# three

Anna rose with the dawn. She'd always risen early, but this was earlier than usual. Last night had been a restless one. She couldn't sleep for wondering how her day would go. Not that she worried. She knew she was a good nurse. She cared about people. She could talk to the patients easily, so she filled all the requirements Dr. Snow had mentioned yesterday. But it was a new challenge, and though Anna had always faced a challenge head-on, she was apprehensive now. She would do her best and surely he could expect nothing else.

Bessie's helper had the fire going in the cookstove. "You're up mighty early, Miss Anna."

Anna smiled. "I'm a bit anxious about my first day of work." She paused. "I'm sorry I don't know your name."

"Delia." The young girl bowed slightly.

"Well, Delia, I imagine we'll get to know each other rather well, don't you suppose?"

"Well, good morning to ye." Bessie looked surprised to see Anna standing by the sink. "The sun is barely up, and here ye are already." Bessie added water to the coffee-pot. "The sunrise was beautiful from my bedroom window. Means there'll be no rain, and that's a good sign for ye."

A few minutes later Anna huddled over the warmth from the stove in the dining room.

Coffee would warm her insides and her hands, too.

"Ye need some warmin' up, I see."

Anna nodded. "This is summer—"

"Aye. That it is, but mornings are always cold, even in summer. The ocean brings a wide variety of weather. The cold breeze comes off the ocean. Takes the sun to warm things up a bit. Ye'll get used to it."

In no time the coffee perked on the stove, and Bessie had potatoes sliced and frying. "It'll be oats this morning, scrambled eggs, bread, and potatoes."

Anna took her coffee out onto the sunporch. Her uniform, stiff from starch, was without wrinkles. The maid had insisted all it needed was a bit of pressing to make it presentable. As Anna looked at the sky waking up from its night of darkness, she prayed: "Lord, I come to Thee as Your child. Please be with me this day. Help me to do Thy will. Help me to be an asset to this community, and to assist Dr. Snow in all ways."

*"Trust in the Lord and he will direct thy paths,"* went through her head. She believed that with all her heart. God directed. God had pointed her in this direction, and He would be here to lean on.

Others came down the stairs and Anna greeted Mr. Webster. He was hard of hearing so she had to raise her voice.

"It's a perfect day, Mr. Webster."

He wore the same shirt and pants he'd had on yesterday, but he'd clipped some of the straggly parts of his beard. "Yes, missy, you're right there. But, then, it's always a perfect day at the beach."

Anna greeted every one, then went to refill her coffee cup. She offered to help bring the food to the table, but Bessie told her to sit down. "I'll handle it with Delia's help." Though Bessie didn't need to serve, she often did so. "I prefer to keep busy and just like to cook" was her comment.

Bessie asked the blessing and everyone dug in. Though her plate was filled with food, Anna found it difficult to swallow. She'd never reacted like this before. Why was the job affecting her this way?

At last it was time to go. Anna put on the navy blue cape and pinned the cap to her hair. One of the helpers had brought the horse and buggy around and helped her up.

"We will see ye at 11:45 sharp," Bessie called from the doorway.

Anna nodded.

It had been a long time since living on the farm, and then she had ridden bareback, but taking the reins, she knew she'd have no problem with this gentle gray horse, as she called to him to giddiyup.

Since Anna had not been to Dr. Snow's home, she could hardly wait to see it. She'd heard it was right close to the center of Long Beach. The large home was the hospital, doctor's office, and waiting room. She was also eager to meet his housekeeper, Lizzie, who lived in, cooked most of his meals, and washed the necessary linens.

A sign revealed she'd arrived at the right house. Anna drove around to the back and a form appeared to take charge of the buggy before she had a chance to light. "Doc Snow told me you were coming," the young boy said. He was not more than ten, Anna decided. She thanked him for his help and went to the front door.

Lizzie, the housekeeper, answered the knock. A short, full-figured woman, she had a warm smile and a firm handshake. "Dr. Snow is in the examining room—two doors down."

Dr. Snow appeared in the hallway. "Miss Galloway. You are earlier than I expected."

Anna tried to read his expression. Was he pleased or not? Perhaps he was not quite ready for her to arrive. "Everything was done that needed doing, so I came on ahead."

"Good. I appreciate both punctuality and efficiency in people. Come. I'll show you around what I call the infirmary."

It was primitive, but better than not having a hospital at all.

The waiting room, which would have been a front room, was rectangular and spacious. Two sofas, two low tables and an occasional table filled the room. An oval throw rug covered the middle of the floor. The walls were a bright yellow.

"Very nice," Anna said. "My sister, Pearl, likes yellow. It does perk one up, don't you think?"

"Hmmm—" Dr. Snow seemed deep in thought. "I had nothing to do with the color. It was like this when I first came."

Anna followed him down the hall into a room with a long, leather-covered table. A desk fit nicely in one corner, and a small table with supplies in another. "My examining room."

"Adequate," was all Anna said. She wasn't about to make any extra comments. Clearly, he was a man of few words.

There was a water closet for patients and another room for minor operations. "We make do with what we have," he said, closing the door of the small operating room.

"I must check on a few patients. You may come with me, or stay here in case someone should need help. What would you prefer?"

Anna wondered if she would usually go with him, or stay in case of an emergency. Dr. Snow put his coat on, then stood, as if waiting for her reply. His eyes seemed to penetrate her and she looked away.

He paused. "Why not come with me—at least for today. I'll use the larger buggy and we'll be off."

Anna felt the stiffness of her uniform as he helped her into the buggy.

"We'll head up to Tioga Station first. I'm treating a man with chilblain. He's going to have to give up working at sea."

"Is that a common problem here?" Anna asked, remembering it was similar to frostbite, but not as severe.

"Yes, afraid so. Charlie works in the cold, damp air. He's getting too old for that—I told him so last month."

They rode on in silence though Anna had a hundred questions rumbling through her mind.

He lifted the reins and paused for a moment. "Of course we'll head back to Bessie's close to noon. This is the day for her bean and ham soup. My favorite!"

Anna smiled as she stared at the doctor's profile. He was like her brothers Ben and Albert—and Jesse, too, she supposed, though she had not seen Jesse in such a long time—always thinking about food, *good food*, that is.

They reached the home, not much more than a shack, and Dr. Snow introduced Anna as the new nurse. Anna shook the hand and smiled, but couldn't help noticing the swelling of the man's hands and feet. His hands were clammy.

"Charlie, find a new job," Dr. Snow said, examining his patient. "You know what I told you—"

"Yes, doctor, but it's what I do. I can't stay indoors."

"He is a fisherman and works through cold and wet," he said, glancing at Anna. "Be careful not to warm up the hands too quickly." He turned back to his patient. "That's what causes the pain and tissue damage. I'll give you salve to help the itching, and stop by next week, okay?"

There was one more stop before they headed back toward town and lunch at the boardinghouse.

"See how busy I am?" His face looked serious, but Anna caught the undertone of sarcasm, or was he in earnest? She did not know how to read him yet.

"The lady over on Shoalwater Bay—the one expecting a baby—I mentioned yesterday."

"Yes, I remember."

"Her husband wants her to go into Portland early, but she doesn't want to. I may get a call some night, but then again, they may deliver it themselves. Her neighbor has been known to assist in deliveries."

Anna enjoyed his sharing his practice with her, his thoughts on the local people and the various diseases and treatments he had given.

"You will undoubtedly see shipwreck victims while you're here. The ships get into rough water, or off course, and come in too close. When they go aground, we can save them, but often the whole crew is swept out to sea, and there's not a thing we can do."

Anna had never tended to a shipwreck victim, though

she had seen a drowning. "I'm certain I can handle any situation," she said. "God brought me here for a reason and I intend to fulfill my life's ambition."

"God." Snow said the name with disdain. "Not sure I believe in God. He took my mother, the only person who loved me and cared about what happened—"

"You have no father?"

"He was busy with his work and had no time for me."

"I'm sorry—"

"Don't be."

Anna moved away as if she'd been touched with a hot poker. Everything had been fine until she mentioned God. She couldn't help but speak of God, as He was very much a part of her life and she couldn't exclude Him from her conversation as if He never existed.

"You don't pray for your patients then?" She had to ask it.

He turned and stared. "No, I never pray for patients. Why should I? It does no good. Weren't you listening to me?"

The words stung, but Anna ignored them. "I pray for patients. Is that going to be a problem, doctor?"

"You do what you want, just don't expect any miracles. We work with what we have and that's about all we can do."

Of course Anna did not agree, but what was the point of arguing? It was a closed subject, and one she chose not to pursue. At least not now. He did not know her yet, nor she him; but there would come a time when Anna's prayers would be heard and answered.

"Do you usually say what's on your mind?"

Anna stiffened. Not one for thinking things out, Anna

had been in trouble more than once for her outspoken-ness. It was because of that, that her mother had ques-tioned her becoming a nurse. "Seems one would need to think, then act," she'd said, "when dealing with people's lives."

Of course Sarah had been right, and Anna had become better at thinking things out, then making a choice. Except for when she had cut her hair.

"You have a nice smile. I think the people will cotton to you just fine."

Anna's cheeks burned. A nice smile, indeed. Joseph had said it was her eyes that were her best feature. It cer-tainly could never be her thick, unmanageable hair. Even short, it did what it wanted to.

"I speak without thinking," Wesley Snow said then, as if reading Anna's mind. "I apologize if I offended you before about your hair."

"It's quite all right." Anna held her head high and thrust her chin forward. If the truth were to be known—but far be it for her to divulge every bit of truth—his statement about God was far more offensive.

They passed the grocery store. Dr. Snow pulled on the reins suddenly. "Just remembered that Lizzie asked me to pick up some salt today. If I don't, my chicken will taste pretty flat."

"Do you want me to purchase it for you?"

He smiled, revealing even, white teeth. "That would be nice."

Anna held her skirts up, assuring Dr. Snow she did not need his assistance in getting down.

The store resembled the mercantile she'd shopped at in Portland. There was a bit of everything and Anna could have looked all afternoon and not seen it all. One thing caught her eye: the candy counter—she should take back some lemon drops for Bessie, and crackers from the cracker barrel for her, but it was lunchtime and Dr. Snow was not a patient man.

"Can I help you with something?" the man behind the counter asked.

"Salt," Anna replied. "It's for Dr. Snow. He says to put it on the account."

The proprietor dug out a receipt box from under the counter, then glanced up. "Say, aren't you the nurse who came from Portland?"

Anna smiled. "That I am." She extended her hand. "Anna Galloway."

His grip was firm. "Name's Fenton. Glad to meet ya. Doc needed someone to help him out since we can't get another doctor to come here."

"It's a great place. I like it very much already."

He brought a huge container of salt. "Is that all?"

Anna nodded and started to leave just as two barefoot children came in. The older one came up, thrusting a penny on the counter. "Licorice, please."

Mr. Fenton handed him two strings of licorice and took the penny. His little brother pointed at the hard candy. "Me eat, me eat."

"And here's a piece of candy for you."

Anna laughed as he poked it into his mouth. Seconds later, drool cascaded down his face, mixing with rivulets of dirt.

Anna saw a copy of *The Oregonian*, and was starting to pay for it when she heard a choking sound. Turning, she dropped the paper and rushed up the aisle as she saw the grubby-faced little boy turning red. His brother stood screaming. Fenton kept saying, "Oh my."

Anna turned the boy upside down and pounded on his back. The piece of hard candy shot across the room, landing on top of the pickle barrel.

The older boy stopped screaming and Fenton clapped his hands.

"Oh my," he repeated. "I do declare. That happened so fast, I was standing there like a dumbbell. I guess you know what you're doing, being a nurse and all."

A lady who had just entered the store stood with gloved hand covering her mouth. "I wouldn't have known what to do. Thank goodness you were here."

Anna set the boy down, ruffling his hair. "You'll be just fine now. Don't try to talk when you're eating, or suck in when eating hard candy."

"He won't no more, ma'am," the older child said, putting his arm around his brother who was still bawling like a newborn calf.

Anna picked up the paper, plunked down a nickel, and asked for five cents worth of lemon drops. "For Bessie," she said.

Fenton pushed the money back to Anna. "You ain't paying for the newspaper or the lemon drops. Not this day!"

Anna left with her salt and other purchases and hurried to the side of the store where Dr. Snow waited.

"What was the screaming about? And what took you so long?"

"Which question should I answer first?" Anna asked, setting the purchases in the back.

He glared. "Tell me about the screaming."

After she relayed the story, he shook his head. "Well, I'll be. He sort of initiated you, didn't he?"

His full mouth turned into a half smile. She suspected he was amused, but she didn't care. She was needed here. She'd done her first act of nursing.

Soon they were on their way. "Tell me," Dr. Snow said, breaking the silence. "What do you think of young Peter Fielding?"

Anna swallowed. "He helped me get settled."

"He needs a wife."

"Bessie told me about Callie."

"You might be the one."

Anna's eyes snapped. "I am a nurse, Dr. Snow. I did not come here to find a husband, if that's what you're thinking."

"Good."

Anna was relieved to see the roof of the boardinghouse over the next road. She'd had enough of this conversation.

"I see a bit of temper in you, Miss Galloway."

"Only when provoked," Anna said, staring straight ahead.

"I believe we have arrived at Bessie's." He didn't look her way. "I'm sure you can put all of this behind you and indulge in the stimulating conversation around the table."

Anna was later to think about that moment, wondering if she could have been fired for her impolite manner before she even got a start at nursing here. Yet, she thought she caught the sound of a chuckle as the groom came up and took the horse to be watered. Could Dr. Snow have been amused by her outburst? Well, her affairs were none of his business or anyone else's. She would behave in a proper fashion, be chaperoned should she be courted, and certainly give it careful thought before ever agreeing to marry anyone. As long as she nursed to the best of her ability, no problems should arise. Of course to marry would mean the end of her career, and Anna enjoyed nursing far too much to give it all up. At least not yet. Not now. . .

## four

The discussion around the table was lively, especially after Dr. Snow reported on what Anna had done.

"Word'll get out," Mr. Webster said. "Our nurse here will be a celebrity."

Anna's cheeks flushed. "Don't be absurd. I did what anyone would do."

"Not so," Bessie said, passing around a plate of cranberry nut muffins. "I don't know if I'd a-done what ye did."

"A nurse is always prepared, right, Miss Galloway?"

*Miss Galloway.* She'd much prefer he call her Anna. Before she had a chance to answer, Bessie said that Peter had brought Ned back and wanted to stop by that evening so Anna could meet his children.

"I'm looking forward to it," Anna said, knowing Dr. Snow was watching her with an I-told-you-so expression. She took a big swallow of coffee, then began choking.

"Here. I'll tend to that." Dr. Snow got up and instead of pounding her on the back, acted as if he was going to lift her and turn her upside down.

"I'm—quite—all right—" Anna ran from the room, coughing into her apron.

When she came back to the dining room, Bessie had a twinkle in her eye, and Mr. Webster asked if she was okay.

"Dr. Snow said you could have the afternoon off. Not

that much going on, it seems."

Anna was relieved. Having not slept well the night before, she knew a nap would help. If the fog lifted, she would walk to the beach and enjoy watching the tide coming in, or going out. She really wasn't sure how one could tell. It looked the same to her.

When Anna wakened from a short respite, she was happy to see the sun was shining. Its warmth filled her room, rejuvenating her. She remade the bed, then donned her cotton stockings.

She couldn't help but be disappointed that Dr. Snow had left without her after lunch. Bessie said he was being kind, thinking she needed her rest, but maybe he didn't want her around. How would she know? He was difficult to understand, and maybe she never would understand men.

Anna gazed at Joseph's photo atop her dresser. A lump came to her throat, as she picked it up and stared into the eyes. Somehow she wasn't quite ready to give him up. Maybe she should return to Iowa, try to see him once again.

The photo went back on the dresser as Anna slipped into her older brown high-tops and grabbed a hat. She'd borrow a cloak from the downstairs closet. "I often have guests who don't come prepared for a walk on the beach," Bessie had said yesterday. "Use any of these things. Anytime."

Anna chose a pair of warm brown woolen gloves. Even with the sun out, the wind could cut right through you.

Anna did not know about the ocean—the waves that sneaked up and drenched you in seconds—waves that carried people out to sea. She might have asked Cora to come, or anyone else, but the dining area was empty and Bessie was nowhere to be seen. It must be rest time, she thought.

The water was close, just beyond a small copse of beach pines. Anna slipped down a well-worn path, her heavy shoes sinking into the sand. Once she hit the water's edge, she was glad she'd worn the heavy coat. The wind whipped around her, making the coat billow out. A thinner wrap would have been torn from her body.

Anna walked along, liking the way the water came in and out, sometimes closer, sometimes nipping at the soles of her shoes. Seagulls swooped down as if looking for a handout. She loved watching their graceful dives. Finally she knew she had to go into the water. It seemed to beckon to her.

Slipping out of the shoes and brown stockings, Anna left them in a pile close to the path and raced back to the water. She ran in, without thinking, then sucked her breath in. The water was icy cold! She hadn't expected it to be this cold. She grimaced and walked further out. Perhaps one got used to it after a bit.

Another wave came, taking her breath away. Anna ran back from the teasing waves. Hearing a shout, she turned her head just as the biggest wave ever came and knocked her off her feet.

Gulping in huge mouthfuls of salt water, Anna tried to gather her bearings, but her dress was thick and now heavy and wet. She struggled just as another wave caught her in its clutches carrying her further out.

"Help!" She finally called, thrusting her head out of the water. "Help!" she called again, just as another wave came and pulled her under. Anna's life passed before her as she felt the water numbing her, taking her breath away. Papa. Mama. Sisters Pearl and Clara, whom she hadn't seen in so long. Albert, Ben, and Jesse. Jesse, her eldest brother, who had deserted his family. Would she ever see him again? Ever be able to tell him she loved him in spite of his orneriness? Emily's face flashed through her mind. She'd grown to love her sister-in-law like a sister in a few short weeks. And Baby Clifford. Who couldn't love his chubby face, the happy smile. There was also Paul, Brother Luke, and Kate. She was pulled under again, her mind saying prayers to her Father above. . . .

A voice shouted. "Here! Catch this!"

Anna felt something go over her head and she realized it was a rope. It anchored her and she felt the comfort of something solid.

"Hold on! We'll pull you ashore."

Having swallowed numerous gulps of salt water, Anna relaxed and let herself be pulled in. Finally she was out of the thrashing water and she sunk into a heap on the ground, breathing huge gulps of air. Another voice joined the first voice, but she was too exhausted to look up, to even thank her rescuer.

"We must get her inside, quick!" Anna felt the warmth of a thick, dry blanket. "It doesn't take long for exposure to set in. My wagon's close at hand."

"Anna! Can you hear me?"

From the depths of her whirling mind, she wanted to say, yes, but all she could do was nod. The voices sounded familiar now.

"Bessie will get her warm in no time."

Anna felt herself being lifted into the wagon. She huddled

closer under the blanket. Then the voice of an angel rang out.

"Anna, oh, Anna, why did you go wading when the tide is going out?" It was Bessie.

Soon she was assisted inside to the sofa in the parlor. Her clothing stuck to her, but Bessie pulled them off her while Cora's voice sounded in the background. "Here are the blankets."

"Good. Now fetch a cup of hot tea."

Anna's teeth began chattering, her hands gripping the edge of the blanket. Hair was pushed out of her face, while Bessie clucked over her.

"Child, I wish ye'd said something about wanting to go wading."

Anna glanced up as Cora placed a cup into her hands. The steam revived her as she breathed deeply of the pepperminty flavor.

"Drink it up," Bessie commanded. "It will bring warmth to the bones."

"Should I go for Dr. Snow?" Cora asked, hovering around the edges.

Bessie shook her head. "She's going to be okay. We got her barely in time. She'll be fine once she warms up. I'll get her in by the fire."

Anna opened her eyes again, but the room seemed to wave around her.

"Anna, don't go to sleep." The cup was taken from her trembling hands. "You must stay awake and talk to me."

"Bessie?" Why was her mind hazy? Why couldn't she focus on Bessie's face?

She was pushed to her feet and pulled into the room by

the huge stone fireplace. "Talk to me," the voice commanded.

"I—" But Anna's teeth chattered so badly she couldn't say anything.

"Here. Sit. I'm bringing some warm beef broth. That may be better than tea."

Anna heard the words "fetch" and "doctor." But she wanted to huddle under the blankets more, wanted to sleep so she wouldn't need to think anymore.

"I lost my husband. I lost my child. I am not losing you, Miss Anna Galloway."

"But I am not a suitable nurse." Could that be her voice? Had she said that?

"O dear, God." Bessie lifted Anna's face, made Anna open her eyes. "Ye are speaking foolishly. I will not hear of it!"

Anna started to slip away, then heard the sound of her father. It was as if he was telling her to go back, to learn, to love. That she was needed here in this place.

She glanced up and finally focused on the older woman's face that bent down, staring at her.

"Anna! You're here. You're back among us! Praise the good Lord!"

Anna slept through dinner. Voices from the dining room table wafted in to her where she lay on the window bench. She strained to hear the words.

"Saved a child's life today, only to need to be saved herself!" Who was that? The voice sounded familiar. Anna lifted up on one elbow and heard another younger voice. Then she knew. Peter Fielding was here. Peter and his children. Her hand went to her hair, as she looked down at some sort of wrap Bessie had put on her. This would never do. She couldn't meet Peter and the children, or any of the boarders looking like this. What a fright she was.

Anna rose from the couch, keeping the blanket around her shoulders as she tiptoed up the steps. If anyone saw her—those sitting at the end could see her—but she had to chance it. Quickly she hurried up the stairs. Once in her room, she stared at her face, still pale from the near-death adventure.

She slipped into clean undergarments and into the blue gingham. It had the fewest amount of wrinkles. She ran a brush through the salt-laden hair and put on clean stockings and the shoes she'd worn on the trip here.

"Oh, Anna, you fool!" she said to her reflection in the mirror. "How can Dr. Snow trust you to care for patients when you can't even take care of yourself?"

Pulling in her breath, her fingers clutched the sides of her dress as she weakly made her way down the steps and to the dining room where people were still eating. Life must go on, and she wasn't going to let one almost drowning accident stop her.

Holding her head high, she entered the dining room and pointed to the large casserole in the center of the table. "I think I'll have a bit of whatever is in that dish."

# five

Peter Fielding stood and helped Anna to a vacant chair. "Quite a day you've had, Miss Galloway. I arrived just in time for dinner, and Bessie told me of your struggle with the tide. Of course I'd already heard about the boy's life you saved at the mercantile."

"You heard?"

Peter nodded. "This is a small town. Everyone knows everyone else's business. This latest part, including your rescue, will also be passed from pillar to post." His eyes were warm, not teasing her as Anna feared.

She looked at the two small faces, then nodded at Mr. Webster, Cora, and the others. "I am just thankful that someone rescued me, since I was beyond rescuing myself."

"I saw ye, missy, from my bedroom window," Mr. Webster offered. "Went down and told Lizzie right off. A neighbor done brought his wagon."

Anna sank deeper into the chair. "It was a dangerous thing to do. I'll not play heedlessly with *that* water again."

"Ye had no way of knowin', and not a-one of us thought to tell you about the dangers of the surf and those huge waves that sweep one right off her feet." Bessie's eyes looked moist.

Peter motioned for his children to stand. "Miss Anna Galloway, this is Catherine and Henry."

Catherine, with a pixie-shaped face, smiled, revealing a gap in her front teeth. "Hello, Miss Galloway." She curtsied. Henry hid his head behind his father's leg, and wouldn't be coaxed into an introduction.

"He's been shy like this ever since Callie—" Peter's face went blank, "that is, his mama died."

Anna nodded, thinking of her own dear mother and how she might have felt if she'd lost her at such a tender age. "It's understandable. He needs time. And how old are you, young man?"

"He's four and I'm six," Catherine answered, flashing another big grin.

Anna had to laugh, remembering when she used to speak for Albert and how angry it made him. Suddenly she remembered the books she'd brought. Reading books, two tablets, and a small box of watercolors. Just the gift for these two. That would come later.

"Ye needs to eat," Bessie said then, "while the rest of us get chocolate cake."

"Chocit cake?" Henry finally found his tongue.

"Yes!" Catherine clapped her hands. "Chocolate is my absolute most favorite cake of all." Her eyes danced with excitement. Anna had a sudden impulse to reach over and pull the motherless girl close. It was apparent that it took very little to please her. It made Anna like her even more.

"Ah, I knew ye would open up to that," Lizzie said with a nod to Henry.

They all sat and talked while Anna ate. Afterwards Anna took her cake and cup of coffee into the living room where she could sit and visit with Peter and his children. Bessie said she did not need to help clear the table, though she offered. Sarah had taught her children to always offer their help, no matter what the situation.

Anna would never forget the words, the sage advice from her mother.

"I'd thought we might go clamming on Sunday. After church, that is." Peter sat across from Anna.

Anna thought of the water, the coldness of it, the gigantic wave taking her out to sea, and fear swept over her. "Clamming? Doesn't that mean we need to be in the water?"

Peter threw back his head and laughed. "Yes. Somewhat. We wait though until low tide, then dig in the high ground."

Panic seized Anna at the memory of only a few hours ago. "I don't think—I'm ready for the beach quite yet."

"Oh, yes, Miss Galloway," Catherine cried. "You must come. We can have a picnic and play ball, and it will be fun."

Peter cast a stern look and she sat down and held her small hands in her lap, but her eyes hadn't lost their sparkle. Peter looked over the top of his daughter's golden head and smiled at Anna.

Anna felt the tentacles of fear closing in. Did she want to do this? Of course if they didn't go until Sunday, she had three days to prepare herself.

As if reading her mind, Bessie explained that low tide meant there'd be no danger of a wave coming anywhere close. "And I have just the thing to pack," she said. "Fried chicken, potato salad, and ginger cookies."

"Bessie, you're an absolute wonder."

"Oh, go on with ye. But what I think ye need to do is go out on the sunporch and enjoy the sunset."

The four trooped outside to watch the glowing colors of a July summer night. The children insisted on sitting one on each side of Anna. They fit into the lawn swing nicely. Peter sat on a wicker chair across from the swing.

"Doesn't a red sunset mean perfect weather for tomorrow?" Anna asked.

"Oh, yes, to the sailor's delight."

"And I must go to work early," Anna said. "Enough time off for me." Anna glanced at Peter while he tied his son's shoe. She liked him. He was kind, and Lizzie said he believed in God, that he hoped some day to find a Christian mother for his two motherless lambs. He was more open than the brooding Dr. Snow. She wondered if he had thoughts of Callie. How tragic to lose a wife at such a young age.

"I am glad you came to our little peninsula," Peter said, his voice husky sounding.

"I'm glad I came, too." Anna's cheeks flushed, but it was dark enough so no one would notice. "Does Dr. Snow ever go clamming?" she asked.

"I don't know, but I doubt that he does. He's far too busy."

"Maybe we should ask him to accompany us," though she knew he'd say no.

An awkward silence filled the porch. "I think teaching one person how to dig is enough for one outing," Peter finally said. "I'll take him another time—if he wants to go, that is."

"It was just a thought," Anna said.

"Someone's got to be there in case of emergencies," Peter added.

"Yes, you're right, I'm sure."

Long after Peter left, Anna thought about the evening, how comfortable she felt around him. It was as if she didn't need to prove herself, as if he liked her just as she was, impetuosity and all. With Dr. Snow it was different. She kept feeling he disapproved of her, no matter how hard she tried. No, it was definitely not a good idea to ask the doctor to go clamming, but Anna wondered if this was the real reason for Peter's comment.

❧

Anna kept busy the remainder of the week. She removed a sliver from a baby's finger—the child would not sit still for the mother—helped set two broken arms—two different people—and assisted in a tonsillectomy.

"Those tonsils are the largest I've ever seen," Dr. Snow had said, holding them up with forceps.

Anna examined the inflamed tissue and nodded. "No wonder this child had sore throat on top of sore throat."

A lady came in to have a boil lanced under her arm. "The herbs I've been taking haven't helped," she explained, looking sheepish.

"Some of the people are superstitious and try old home remedies first," Dr. Snow said after she'd left. "I'm hoping my presence will prevent needless deaths.

"Speaking of deaths," Dr. Snow smiled at Anna. "I heard about a certain someone who let a wave knock her down."

Anna's face flushed.

"It's okay. You weren't forewarned. You saved that boy's life, earlier, so it was your turn to be saved."

"Yes, my guardian angel was watching out for me."

Dr. Snow scoffed, "It was George Webster who saved your life. Who knows what might have happened if he hadn't been looking out his window."

"Well, that may be true, but still—" Anna saw the tight-lipped look and decided to drop it. She believed that God often sends His messengers to intervene, but there was no convincing a person who didn't wish to believe. But Anna knew and would always believe that's what happened on that sunny afternoon in July.

"By the way, almost forgot. I have something for you."

"For me?"

"Yes. From the child's parents. His family was most appreciative and dropped by with a dozen eggs and a plate of homemade cinnamon rolls."

"What?" Anna exclaimed. "I expected no pay."

"That's how these people are. You cannot do them a good turn without their repaying you for your troubles."

Anna thought of the stack of unpaid bills in the file. People who could not pay. People who might never pay. Yet Dr. Snow would attend to their needs. She knew he'd never turn anyone away.

His manner was abrupt, but she could handle that. The main thing was the concern he showed for his patients. She noticed that right off that first day. Always curt with her, he turned on the charm for the next patient he saw.

That afternoon he nodded and smiled as he listened to a lady complain about her aches and pains.

"Comes with old age, Miss Connors."

She laughed. "I thought you'd say that, doctor."

He turned to Anna after the woman left. "The people are friendly, but set in their ways. Even if I offer advice, they go ahead and do what they've always done."

"Yes, I find it to be so," Anna said, "and I've only been here a short while."

She assisted Dr. Snow, often anticipating, even suggesting a possible treatment. Once he had barked, "And who is the doctor here?"

Her cheeks had flamed as she hurried from the room. Her boldness had gotten her into trouble before; she couldn't let it happen now. She blew her nose in the empty waiting room, and tried to appear busy as she thumbed through the stack of charts on the various patients. Most names meant nothing to her. But they would, she vowed.

The remainder of the week, Dr. Snow seemed withdrawn, more brusque than usual. Perhaps it had to do with Lucinda, his betrothed.

Lizzie, the housekeeper, had brought up her name the day before. "That woman is the most spoiled I've seen and I've certainly run into a few in my day."

"Lucinda?"

Lizzie stopped dusting. "They are to be married next June, when he moves back to Portland."

"Move? He's going to move? I thought he liked it here."

"I know, my dear girl, but Lucinda does not, and Lucinda is used to having her own way."

Anna wanted to question Dr. Snow about it, but thought better of it. Perhaps he did need to go back to Portland to practice, but what would the people do then? They depended on his knowledge and most every one liked him. He put on a different face for patients as opposed to other people.

"I think he's in a snit because she's coming in November."

"She's coming here?"

"Why does that surprise you? She'll travel the same way you did, I expect. Probably come with a friend or a chaperone, though Lucinda certainly does not need a chaperone."

"She's come before?"

"Oh, my yes. Came last spring. Thought there might be a wedding in the new Methodist Episcopal Church not too far from the boarding house, but Lucinda soon let it be known she wanted to be married in a *huge* church with eight attendants."

"You know her well?"

Lizzie turned and stared at Anna. "I guess you didn't know."

"Know? Know what?"

"I used to be the cook for Lucinda Lawson's folks. I believe her mama sent me here to keep an eye on Dr. Snow."

"I had no idea."

"You don't need to go a-talking about it—though of course Bessie knows. Between us, we keep an eye on the good doctor, though more that he be fed right, rather than the fact that he might have a roving eye. Not that he'd have time for it, anyway!"

Anna knew that to be true. Dr. Snow rarely had a day off. There was always someone else to see, to "fix up better than new" as he always said.

"I'd never talk about Dr. Snow," Anna said then. "I do not believe in spreading rumors. You can trust me to keep my lip buttoned up."

Lizzie leaned over and impulsively hugged Anna. "I only been here a year, mind you, but I care for that man as if he were my own son. What he needs is to find is someone like you, Miss Anna."

Anna laughed. She wasn't quite right for the good doctor. Besides, she wasn't looking for a man to marry. She gave Lizzie an impulsive hug. "I'm going to keep right on a-doing what I do the best: nursing."

Horses drew up to the side of the house. Dr. Snow had returned from his morning schedule. Anna busied herself by rearranging the bandages and medicines on the shelf. No wonder he had been agitated. Maybe he wanted to marry, but she also knew doctoring was his work and he preferred a small town. Would Miss Lucinda ever come to realize that?

The door opened. He rushed in and as Anna looked up, their eyes met. It was the first time she'd noticed an emotion other than a businesslike one. There was almost a kindness in his expression, before he turned and looked away.

"Stopped by to see if you're wanting to go to Bessie's—pick up lunch."

"I brought my lunch today. If you don't mind, I'll stay here, just in case—"

"Whatever you do is entirely up to you, Miss Galloway." He strode past her, muttering something as he refilled his medicine bag with supplies. "Whatever you do is entirely up to you. I'll be back presently."

Lizzie appeared in the doorway. "Thought I'd prepare a meat loaf, if you think you'd like that for the evening meal."

He paused, then stared at her strangely. "Lizzie, you know I eat whatever you fix and half the time don't taste it anyway. Not that it's your fault. It's just the way I am by the end of the day—being tired and all."

Anna busied herself with the charts, pretending she hadn't heard. She knew the feeling. She'd been so busy in nursing school that it didn't matter what she ate. Her friends often had to coax her to come to the table during meals. There were always other more important things to do.

"I'll be back." Again the door opened and he was gone. Anna lifted her shoulders and told her heart to slow down. She had no idea why Dr. Wesley Snow had looked at her in such a way. His bold look had mesmerized her— at least for the moment.

It was time for lunch. She'd visit more with Lizzie Myles. It seemed she knew as much about the goings-on as Bessie McGruder. Suddenly Anna had an urge to find out more about Miss Lucinda Lawson, especially since she'd be coming soon. Perhaps her presence would make Dr. Snow smile more. He had such a nice, warm smile when he smiled. She wished she knew what made him so unhappy, so full of negative thoughts. Not knowing God as she did had some bearing, but it seemed to go further than that. Yes, perhaps Lucinda Lawson was just what the doctor needed.

## six

Sunday morning boasted a blue sky without a trace of the usual wispy white clouds that drifted across in lazy fashion. Anna bounded from bed, eager to attend the small church two blocks south of the boardinghouse. It was Methodist Episcopal, the one Bessie said Dr. Snow would be married in, should Lucinda change her mind and move to the peninsula. Anna had never been Methodist, but it didn't matter. To be attending the service meant so much. She loved to sing hymns and to pray amongst friends. The oft-quoted verse came to mind: "Whenever two or more are gathered in my name, there I am also."

She chose her best rose pink chambray with a delicate white lace collar and a touch of lace at the cuffs. The skirt was full, the waistline accented by eight pleats. It was clearly her best dress next to the sea green taffeta, the maid-of-honor dress Kate had made for Pearl's wedding in Portland. Anna was saving that for a special day.

Anna brushed her short locks until the hair shone. She found a tiny bit of ribbon that matched the dress, and pinned it on one side. There. She had taken so long fussing with her hair and dressing, in between looking out her window, marveling in the beauty of the day, she was late to breakfast.

"Now this is the kind of summer day I am used to," Anna said, as she hurried to the table to dish up the last portion of scrambled eggs.

Mr. Webster glanced up from his plate of toast. "And isn't it today you're going a clamming?"

Anna's heart sank. "Yes, we'll leave right after church." She was not looking forward to digging clams, but the children were so excited, she must be happy for their sake.

Bessie smiled. "Bless Peter's heart. He knows how I love clam fritters and chowder."

Anna took her second cup of coffee into the living room. She liked sitting on the window seat with its view of the ocean. Though it terrified her now, she would never tire of the frothy waves coming and going. It reminded her of God's might in creating something so huge, so powerful.

She set the cup aside and reached for her Bible. The leather of Sarah's worn Bible was soft.

She turned to Isaiah 30. "In quietness and in confidence shall be your strength." *In quietness.* Wasn't that why it was good to go off to a quiet spot to read, to pray?

It was now nearing nine. The service was at ten. Peter said to expect him at nine-thirty.

"You certainly look pretty." Cora slipped into the room and sat across from Anna.

"Why, thank you, Cora. Would you like to come to church with us?"

The small girl shook her head. "No, thank you. I am Catholic, you know, but I rarely attend Mass. Still, once a Catholic, always a Catholic."

"Oh." Not that it mattered to Anna. She thought it most important that all people believed in God. They could attend any church they wanted to. Sarah had instilled a deep and abiding love for God in all of her children. All believed, with the possible exception of Jesse, who had left his family and, as far as Anna knew, was still wandering hither and yon, falling in and out of love, making others completely miserable.

"Some children never grow up," Sarah had said about her firstborn.

But Anna, determined at a young age to always do what was right, to follow God in spite of the circumstances, now was living away from everyone, in this primitive spot that only a pioneer could love. Yet God wanted her here; she was very sure of that.

Anna'd been so busy working, busy thinking and worrying about others, she'd had little time for God. Now with a day off, she wondered what it would be like to be entirely free. Not that anyone was ever free. Still, she knew one must make time to read the Scriptures, for prayer, for contemplation. Since she'd come, she'd contemplated much, wondering what God wanted of her. Was nursing to be the way her life was spent, or did He have something else in store for her? Whichever, Anna felt blessed and open to God's way. She bowed her head.

"Lord, I pray for Peter and his children, for those who are sick, for Dr. Snow that he might believe again.

"And am I blessing You God? Am I doing what You would have me do? I feel Your presence as I work each day. I am grateful for that—truly I am. . ."

The sound of horses hooves filled the still morning air. Anna closed her Bible and rose from the couch. The carriage pulled up out front, and from the sides, hands waved, voices shouted.

Peter came to the door, but Anna opened it before he could knock. His dark suit and red tie nearly took her breath away. She'd never realized how truly handsome he was. His eyes lingered on hers for a long moment.

"You look lovely in that pink dress, Anna." His eyes had an intense look, making Anna feel self-conscious.

"Thank you, Peter," she finally murmured. She flushed, but knew he couldn't see it as she went out the door ahead of him. Was pink her color? Not that she'd ever thought about such frivolous things before.

The children greeted her. Henry wore a suit he had outgrown and Catherine looked sweet in a yellow dotted Swiss. A battered straw hat sat atop the blond curls.

"I am so happy to see you," Anna said, squeezing first one pair of hands, then the other. It was then she realized she'd forgotten gloves. Tucked in the trunk still, she had meant to wear them, as proper ladies always wore gloves. Even Catherine wore gloves.

"Peter," she touched his shoulder. "I forgot my gloves. I'll be right back."

They were dark gloves, not ones for a summer day; still they were better than bare hands, Anna determined as she ran back down the stairs and out the door to the waiting carriage.

"I want to sit by you in church, Miss Galloway," Catherine said.

"Me, too," piped up Henry.

"Yes, you, too," Anna said.

"And what about me?" Peter raised an eyebrow.

"You can sit on the end, Daddy," Catherine said.

The church was small with wood plank floors, no stained-glass windows, but there was a warmth to it and Anna was happy to note the piano in one corner. A slender blond woman went to the front and sat down to play.

Soon her fingers rippled up and down the keyboard and Anna was enthralled as she hummed "What a Friend We Have in Jesus."

Anna remembered the church she'd attended in Iowa City. She'd wished that Mama could have heard the music, as she loved music so much. But then she'd found the Friend's Church in Portland.

The Reverend Keating, a tall thin man with a warm, engaging smile looked out over his congregation and led them in an opening prayer. Anna liked him immediately, and knew she would come back to this church.

As Anna sat, listening to the sermon, she had to stifle her laugh as first Henry then Catherine squirmed. It was hard to sit still. They'd be more than ready for a trip to the beach.

After church, going back to Bessie's so Anna could change and pick up the lunch, the four headed up north toward Tioga Station, where Peter said the clams were more abundant.

"I brought shovels, buckets, extra coats, blankets, hats, gloves, a lantern, all the things one needs for a clam-digging expedition."

Anna felt overdressed in her old gray muslin, the heavy cloak Bessie insisted she would need, warm cotton stockings, and high-top shoes Bessie had also found.

"Don't want ye catching cold now."

As they started out, Anna chatted to the children, listening to Henry's story about the kitten he had found the day before.

"Did someone abandon it?" Anna asked.

"Ab-abdom?" he asked, screwing up his face.

"You know—leave him alone?"

"He was awfully hungry," Catherine offered. "We named him Fluffy."

"Because he has lots of fur?" Anna asked, her laugh filling the air.

"No, because he had none," Peter said, joining in.

Anna turned to stare at Peter. "You aren't serious, are you?" Her eyes were solemn. "I don't know if I could nurse a cat back to health. They aren't quite like people—"

It was Peter's turn to laugh. "No, he's a fine kitten; a bit skinny, but we can fix that up in no time."

"I don't know how to cook clams—" Anna said as she remembered what the outing was for.

"Don't worry. It's easy. First off, you have to clean them, then fix them."

"You'll show me?"

"Of course."

Now as they headed for what Peter termed the "best spot" Anna felt a sudden chill from a gust of wind that blew up from the ocean. She shivered, remembering her misadventure earlier that week. "The water is never warm in the ocean?" she asked. "Not even in August?"

Peter shook his head. "No. Never."

"But in Iowa the rivers and lakes are warm in the summer."

"They don't move like that, do they?" Peter asked, looking out over a wave smashing against an outcrop of rocks.

"No, guess not."

Anna had learned in the short time she'd been here that most people lived on what they gleaned from the ocean, the bay, and the rivers. Oysters fat and succulent, clams, crabs, salmon, sturgeon. Anna couldn't begin to remember all the things she'd heard. She'd never seen such huge fish as the mammoth salmon and sturgeon. In Iowa, fish were smaller, and bonier.

"Anna! Will you play tag with us?"

She turned and smiled. "Of course. What is all that sand for if we can't play tag. But it will have to be after I catch some clams."

"Dig for clams," Peter corrected her.

"Oh, yes. I keep forgetting."

Peter glanced at the profile of the woman he admired so much. Happy, energetic, she was always ready for the occasion, and the children adored her.

The beach was crowded. The tide was right, as Peter explained, and clams would be plentiful.

"We look for these bubbles in the sand," he explained, kicking at the sand with the tip of his boot. "When you see the bubbles, you start digging as fast as you can."

"As fast as I can?"

"How else will you get the clam?" Peter said.

"I—don't know."

"The clam tries to get away. It isn't stupid. It feels the movement—I guess that's what happens—and starts to burrow deep into the sand. We have to be faster and dig him out."

"How many can we get?"

"As many as we want. I usually stop at fifty."

"Fifty!" Had Anna heard right? "Surely you don't mean fifty."

"Why not?"

"But what do you do with fifty?"

"After cleaning, we can eat them fresh, chop them for chowder, eat more fresh, give some away. I promised Doris

I'd bring her twenty or so." He leaned on the shovel, gazing at Anna for a long moment.

"But, how big are these clams?"

"You've never seen one?"

Anna shook her head. "I grew up in Iowa, remember?"

"But you've seen pictures."

"If I have, I've forgotten." She stared right back.

"Well, well, this will be challenging since you don't know what the thing looks like you're digging for."

Anna started to giggle. "I'll watch you dig for one first. Get an idea of how it goes."

"Okay."

They'd brought blankets for the children to lie on when they tired of playing in the sand. Catherine wanted to dig, but her father said she wouldn't be strong or fast enough. "These critters are smart," he concluded.

The lunch, blankets, lantern, and extra coats and hats were far up on the ridge of grass where the children were told to stay. "You can play in the sand next time. Now you will just get in the way. Go!" He pointed.

Anna watched while they turned and trotted back fifty feet or so.

Peter was fast. In ten minutes he'd dug six clams.

"And I'm supposed to be that fast?" Anna cried.

"Sure. I know you can do it. You work with your hands all the time. You just scoop them out like so."

It was backbreaking work, but Anna finally got her first clam. She held it up and laughed. "See!"

"Put it in the bucket, Anna."

She dug fast and hard, but ended up with just five when it was time to quit.

"I can't believe you got that many," she said, looking

into the bucket with the strange bivalves stacked like so many pancakes on a plate.

"Takes practice. You'll do better next time."

Anna wasn't sure there would be a next time. Her skirts were wet and sandy and her hands cold because she'd discarded the gloves right off. It was too difficult digging with them on.

Anna was right about maybe never digging for clams again when she discovered later just how hard it was to clean them.

Sand and water was everywhere. The little buggers had a ton of sand in them and Peter said it had to come out. If not, the chowder or fried clams would have the gritty sand in them and nobody could eat sand.

"This is more work than the digging," Anna said.

"I know, but you're doing a great job."

Peter said Bessie would show her how to fry them for dinner that night.

Shortly after she had cleaned the clams, doing as Peter showed her, Anna felt the muscles pulling in her back. It had been hard work. Very hard work. She guessed she'd have to go to back to nursing tomorrow to rest up.

## seven

The clams were delicious. Anna decided they were well worth the work of digging, then cleaning them. Bessie was pleased, as were the rest of the boarders.

Anna couldn't wait to tell Dr. Snow about the excursion the day before, and had brought enough for a meal for Lizzie to cook.

"I had an emergency yesterday," Dr. Snow said, ignoring Anna's comment.

"You did?"

"False labor. Mrs. Clayborne."

"Oh. Did you talk her into going across the river to the hospital?"

He glanced at Anna for a long moment. "She's a stubborn woman. Figures since she had Edward without a hospital, this one will be the same."

"And you think not?"

"I know not."

Anna let it drop. Sometimes she felt he was patronizing her. It was much better to keep quiet, to do what she knew how to do.

He left to go on calls, and Anna stayed behind. She wondered if Lizzie knew anything more about Lucinda, if she was still planning on coming.

"Yes, I am sure she is." She shook her head as she cut the clams into long strips. "It isn't good for a couple to be separated. The good doctor is brooding about this. As for

Lucinda, doubt that she has ever not gotten her way, so time will tell."

Anna went with Dr. Snow to Bessie's for lunch. She later wished she hadn't. As they sat over dessert—a fresh plum crisp—the talk revolved around the appendix, how many had burst causing far too many deaths. "All because the symptoms are never recognized," Dr. Snow said. "The appendix is an unknown entity. One never knows why or when an attack will come on."

"Oh, but there are signs," Anna broke in. "Continual abdominal pain, sometimes a fever—"

"I know, Miss Galloway, but how many folks around here pay attention to some little pain or a fever?"

"That might be true, but isn't it our job to educate them?" she continued. "As far as I'm concerned, far too many die from a burst appendix, all because the symptoms are never recognized. Perhaps we should remove the appendix as a precaution—"

"And perhaps you, as a nurse, should leave diagnosing to doctors."

Anna flushed a deep red. "It distresses me is all."

"At least we know when we have smallpox or measles on our hands," Mr. Webster stated, as if wanting to take Anna's side. Anna wondered if Dr. Snow would make further comment on Mr. Webster's observation. She said nothing as she savored the last spoonful of crisp.

Dr. Snow pushed his chair back. "We must go back." He headed out the door with Anna following.

"I expect people don't realize how lucky they are to have a doctor who comes right to their door and administers to them," Anna said, wanting to appease him.

Dr. Snow's jaw was tight, his hands gripping the reins.

"*Luck* is hardly the word for it."

"Well, you know what I mean."

"I'm not a saint," Wesley Snow snapped. "I'm just doing my job."

"As I will do mine," Anna added, staring straight ahead.

The remainder of the trip was spent in silence. The clip-clopping of the horse's hooves was like a song going through Anna's mind. *You will be tolerated. . .you will be tolerated. . .you will be tolerated. . .*

Later, when Anna talked with Bessie, she sighed. "I find it difficult working with Dr. Snow." They sat in the living room, in comfortable chairs looking out toward the ocean and darkening sky as a storm threatened.

"Why is that, child?"

"I'm far too outspoken. Such as this afternoon."

"Fiddlesticks! That's been forgotten for sure."

"I don't think so, Bessie." Anna straightened her shoulders. "He barely spoke to me all afternoon. Then there's the fact that he doesn't believe in God—"

Bessie looked Anna in the eye. "I've known Wesley since the day he arrived. He stayed right here for a month before the house was ready for him. We had lots of talks, and he believes in God, though he may not want to admit it. He's been hurt, that's all."

"Nor does he believe in miracles when it comes to people being healed."

"That may be, Anna, but ye have enough faith for the two of ye."

"He would barely speak to me this afternoon on the rounds." She had tried to get him to talk about himself, but there'd been nothing but silence.

"He just may not understand ye yet. You didn't ask about his life, now did, ye?"

"If you mean about Lucinda—no. I know he's a bear where she's concerned."

"There's the answer. If he offers it, listen, but don't ever pry. He don't open up to no one, probably not even that wife-to-be of his, either."

"I'll never pry, Bessie." Anna knew she could find a job no matter where she went, but she already liked it here. It made her think of home—the small town where everybody was friendly and knew everyone else. In Portland, not one soul smiled when she went to the grocery store. This was beautiful land. She wanted to stay. She wanted to belong. And she hoped Wesley would find her satisfactory.

"Actually, I think he admires ye," Bessie said.

"Never." In spite of her denial, Anna's cheeks reddened. "I did not come here to be admired. I came to help."

"And so ye are." Bessie folded her arms. "Then there's Peter."

"Peter?"

"I can see how he feels about ye."

Anna bristled. "He needs a mother for his children."

"There are worse things than being needed."

After bidding Bessie good night, Anna went to the small room on the second floor, ran water from the reservoir into the small enamel basin, and washed her short locks with rainwater, as there was certainly no shortage of water here. Her thoughts turned to Peter. He had a troubled face and she knew he must be lonely since his wife's death. She wanted to be his friend, but doubted her feelings could go any deeper than that. Still, as Bessie said, one never knew for sure.

Later when Anna went to her room, she got to her knees.

"I pray for wisdom, God. For knowing when to talk and what to say, and for knowing when to listen. Help me be a good nurse. More important, help me to be useful to one and all. Amen."

Anna overslept the next morning. It was all because of the dream. She rarely remembered her dreams, but in this one she found Dr. Snow telling her to go and never come back. Her cheeks were wet with tears when she finally opened her eyes and realized where she was, in the little bed on the top floor with the slanted ceiling, and wallpaper with red rosebuds. Home. This was home now and she was thankful it had been only a dream.

When Anna entered the kitchen, she saw the dirty dishes and silverware in the sink. "You've already eaten?"

"Now don't you fret. Here." Bessie handed her a cup of steaming coffee, then a plate she'd kept in the warming oven. "I didn't waken ye, child, as I figured ye must need your rest."

Anna leaned over, and with one arm, hugged Bessie. "Oh, Bessie, you're so caring and loving. God has blessed you in a mighty way, and me for knowing you."

Bessie nodded. "Aye, I like to think I am doing what the captain would have wanted, but I sure miss his robust laugh, his hearty appetite, the way he could spin a yarn."

Anna thought of the captain and all the others who had drowned in the Pacific Ocean. There would be more shipwrecks. Hadn't the doctor said that yesterday? She hoped there would be survivors. She didn't want to think about sailors drowning and leaving loved ones behind.

Foregoing her second cup of coffee, Anna reached for her cape and cap. "I will see you at lunch." She wanted to ask Bessie what the soup would be, but knew that Dr. Snow knew and would be happy to tell her.

Lizzie met her at the doorway. "You're to meet the doctor at the Claybornes' cabin. There's to be a baby soon."

"The Claybornes' cabin? But where is that? I don't know my way around yet."

"It's down past all the houses." She pointed north. "About a quarter of a mile, or pert' near that far—there's a fence on the ocean side—you turn right there and go until you see his horse and buggy. Now go!"

A birth! Anna liked nothing better than to welcome a new baby into the world. It was one of God's best moments and a joyous occasion for the family. She hoped Dr. Snow's concerns were for naught and that all would be well.

She followed Lizzie's directions—surprisingly—and found the horse and buggy at the front of the house. A small child stood in the open door and clapped when he saw her.

Anna hopped down and hurried inside. The woman was moaning and writhing in the bed. "I can't stand anymore pain, doctor. Oh, please, please do something!"

Dr. Snow glanced up and shook his head. "I thought you'd be here before this."

Anna did not mention she had overslept. The woman cried out and Anna leaned over and held her hand as another contraction hit.

The neighbor acting as midwife looked scared. "I been

here all night long," she offered. "Nothin's happening."

"It must be a big baby," Anna said.

"Breech birth." Dr. Snow nodded.

"What're you going to do?" Anna remembered seeing a cesarean section performed at the hospital in Iowa City.

The woman cried out again. Anna took her hand and stroked her arm. "It's going to be okay. Try to relax."

The woman looked from Anna to her neighbor, then over at Dr. Snow until the next contraction seemed to rip her apart. The woman's fingernails dug into Anna's palm. Another contraction came immediately and another, but it was no use. The child could not come through the birth canal.

"Anna." Dr. Snow motioned toward a corner of the room. "We must operate."

"But we can't take the baby. Not here. There's not enough light, no supplies—"

The frown deepened. "To not do surgery means sure death, probably for both her and the child; to try the surgery could mean death, also."

"We need to transport her to your home."

"There isn't time, Anna."

"But—"

"We'll use the kitchen. It has more light. I'll help Mr. Clayborne move his wife to the table, then you can assist me while the midwife takes care of the chloroform."

Fear rose in Anna's throat. To operate here—under the poorest of conditions—seemed ludicrous, but Dr. Snow was right. They could not stand by and do nothing. It could mean death to both child and the mother.

Dr. Snow began issuing orders. "I'll need boiling water. Towels. Chloroform, antiseptic, my instruments."

Minutes later, Mrs. Clayborne lay on the sheet-covered table, sedated. Anna made a swath with the antiseptic on the woman's stomach. While handing the instruments over, Anna prayed that it wouldn't be too late for the child.

Anna wiped Wesley's forehead as he made an incision through the abdomen, then the uterus.

Mrs. Clayborne moaned.

"More chloroform!" he barked at the midwife. "She must stay sedated." Anna watched as he lifted the baby from the womb, then handed it to her, the umbilical cord following it. He cut it and nodded. "Here, take the baby."

Anna cleaned the mucus from the mouth and made the baby cry.

"Thank God, she's alive," the midwife said, bringing the small basket lined with yellow flannel in from the bedroom. "We'll set this close to the stove."

"A little girl," Anna said, holding the baby close. As her maternal instincts surfaced, Anna realized once again the miracle of birth. A longing filled her as she wondered if she'd ever experience this blessing.

"Anna," Dr. Snow's voice broke through her thoughts. "We have things to do. Let the midwife take care of her now."

Anna handed the tiny baby over, knowing the midwife would wash her off and wrap her in a blanket.

"Yes, sir." Anna moved to the table, and assisted Dr. Snow as he delivered the afterbirth and sutured the woman's abdomen.

Mrs. Clayborne lay still amongst the blood-soaked sheets as Anna cleaned up. Her husband's voice called out. "I heard a baby cry. Is it okay to come in now?"

"In a moment," Anna said, going to the doorway. "We'll make the bed up in there and you can help move her back. And, yes, you have a little girl. She's got a nice, pink color, so it looks as if she'll be fine."

There was another cry and the midwife held the child up. "I think she wants to nurse already."

Mrs. Clayborne moaned again, and Anna administered a bit more chloroform.

"That should do it," Dr. Snow said. "She'll come around soon."

"I couldn't stand it if anythin' happened to her, doctor," Mr. Clayborne said, taking his wife's limp hand.

"I understand, Mr. Clayborne." Dr. Snow looked at the worried husband and new father. "You must make certain she stays in bed. I hope you have someone who can stay with her."

"Maybe Nellie here can stay. Do you suppose?"

The midwife nodded. She'd put the baby back in her bed, and watched her with a smile on her face.

An hour later as the baby slept, Mrs. Clayborne was transferred back to the bedroom, and Dr. Snow was leaving to visit a patient further north. Anna took one more peek at the precious bundle in the yellow-lined basket, then stepped out into the late morning sun.

"What's yore name?" the little boy asked, following Anna outside.

"Anna." She leaned down and ruffled his hair.

"I think our new baby should be named Anna. I like that name, don't you, Pa?"

Mr. Clayborne came out and paused for a moment before going to the barn. "Yes, Edward, I think that's a right nice name."

Anna had never had a baby named for her, not as far as she knew.

"It's a good thing it wasn't a boy, then, because nobody wants to be called Wesley," Dr. Snow quipped, pausing before climbing into the buggy.

Anna left after making sure there was nothing else to be done. The birth had been a pure miracle, and the little one appeared healthy though she'd been through a lot. The first twenty-four hours were the most important.

As she drove back toward town, she felt thankful that Dr. Snow had decided to operate, even under the most primitive of conditions. If they'd waited much longer, little Anna probably would have been dead; the mother, too. She wished they could ride together and discuss the operation he'd performed, but there would be time for that later on. Lunch was out of the question, but Anna didn't feel hungry, anyway.

A bright sun burst out of the thin layer of clouds. Anna thanked the Lord for the day, for His creation, for the sweet-smelling air. What a story she'd have to tell Bessie. Not only the birth of the little girl, but she now had a namesake.

# eight

Dr. Wesley Snow left his last patient at dusk. He would arrive home long after darkness fell, but it was a fine night. No rain. Clear skies. He would enjoy the ride.

Once home, he handed his hat and coat to Lizzie and sat on the sagging couch in the waiting room. A child had vomited on it last week, and though Lizzie had cleaned it, the sour smell lingered.

Things looked dismal. Perhaps Lucinda had been right to leave him, to urge him to return to Portland. Busy with his practice, tending to the small population of the North Beach Peninsula, he would have very little time to attend to her needs. If it hadn't been for Lizzie Myles and the boy he had hired to care for the stable, he would not have a clean house or prepared meals. He looked forward to the noon lunch at Bessie's, but after a hard day of doctoring, he didn't care if he ate or not.

The house was cold and he shivered. He'd had an eighteen-hour day. Nobody should have to work that long, "at least not anybody in their right mind," according to Lucinda.

Stretching out on the couch, he closed his eyes. He imagined he could smell Lucinda's fragrance. She liked rose perfume, and its smell lingered long after she left a room.

"Doctor, would you like the roast from yesterday's dinner, or shall I fix you something else?" Lizzie asked, after entering the room.

He waved her away. "Lizzie, I don't need you fussing over me. Go on and do what you want. I'll be fine."

She left the room, clicking her tongue as she did when she was perturbed with him.

Finally, he rose and went to his room to find his house shoes. The wardrobe held very little. There simply had not been time to shop before moving here a year ago.

He thought again of Lucinda with the sparkling eyes and the tinkling laugh—so different from Anna. Anna's laugh filled a room.

Anna. He had promised himself he would not think of her. His thoughts turned to her, he feared, because he was lonely. Because he wanted to share his life with someone—someday. Because, well, she could make him angry with her professional mannerisms. The big city was still in her, and the people they served were not big city with highfalutin ways. And yet there was an endearing quality about her. Honest and forthright completely. One knew where he stood with Anna.

Yet there was something else. Thoughts of Anna with that wild, unmanageable hair, the gaze that sometimes lingered when she thought he wasn't looking. The warm smile only tormented him, made his heart ache even more deeply. He wanted what he could not have and he'd learned as a young boy how futile that was. His mother dying with the fever—his father standing over her, wringing his hands—praying to God to spare her life.

Wesley had a sister. He knew his father would have wanted more children, had his mother lived, but when she died the light went out in him and he had little time or concern for his children.

It had been a lonely existence. The sister, Helen, was fifteen and soon left to marry a local farmer. After Helen and her new husband moved to Montana to homestead, Wesley was more alone than before.

"Help Father to talk to me," he had prayed in earnest. But even greater was his prayer to learn medicine, to know what to do for sick people, to help them get well, to continue learning about all the cures. Wesley read. What else was there to do? His father, a watch repairman, kept busy in the little shop in front of the house. Winters were cold in Michigan. Bitter. Wesley excelled in school, and nights, after doing his work for the next day, he would read for hours, often until dawn slipped up over the hill in back of the house. Once his father complained about the lamp oil, so Wesley started working at the local mercantile on Saturdays so he could pay for lamp oil and more books.

After graduating from high school and going on to college—at least his father hadn't minded that—reading gave him the opportunity to become even more reclusive. Wesley finished in three years and went on to medical school. Always, forever was the picture of his mother in his mind, with a long braid down her back. He had all but forgotten happy times when they had talked and laughed. His memory, now tattered, was of her lying in bed, moaning, tossing, and turning as the wicked disease claimed her life. Didn't God know that he needed her? That Helen needed her? It hadn't seemed fair and a bit of him died the day his mother was buried in the cemetery west of town.

After graduate school, Wesley went to Oregon. A former classmate, and good friend, had moved to Portland, opened up a practice, and invited Wesley to come join in.

"There is an opportunity to practice what you've learned,

Wes. Come on. I have space for you. There's a need here in Portland, a booming, growing town. You can leave the snow and cold winters behind. Here all it does in the winter is rain."

And so Wesley, with clothes packed in one suitcase, his beloved books in another, boarded a train and traveled to the Northwest.

He had stopped to tell his father good-bye, but received the usual reception. Wesley knew his father wouldn't live forever. His shoulders bent from so many years of bending over watches, the straggly wisps of gray hair nearly broke his heart, but he had to leave. His father had always managed without anyone and would continue to do so.

"I'll write with my address," he said, hugging the old man briefly.

"I won't answer, you know." He looked back at his work and the conversation was over. Wesley had been dismissed as if he was one of the customers. No, the customers received more from his father than he ever had.

Wesley was so busy getting set up in the office he shared with Robert that he found little time for other pleasures.

One Friday after Robert had closed the small office on Woodstock, he eased into his chair and motioned for Wesley to sit, also. "You know, my friend, I never meant for you to come and do all the work. Not only do you see several patients a day, go to homes, and visit those who cannot come here, you do the books, light the fire each morning, and well, good gracious, when are you ever going to find time to relax?

*Relax?* Wesley didn't know about relaxing. He had never known about relaxing. How did one go about doing that anyway when there were more sick people to see, calls in the night, the office to ready for the next day's customers?

"I want you to meet my sister's friend. She's a beautiful woman—loves parties and people. She'll do all the talking. Believe me, you need to do something besides be around sick people."

In the end Wesley had agreed to meet Lucinda Mae Lawson.

Lucinda had a way about her. She drew him out of his shell and ended up being the one whom everybody watched and listened to.

He knew he would never forget the emerald-green dress she'd worn at their first meeting. He fell in love that night. Fell in love with her gaiety, her smile, the way she coaxed a few words from him.

"Come, Wesley, you must dance with me," she'd trilled, pulling on his arm. "It's really quite easy."

He loved the looks of her, the fragrance of roses, her bubbly personality. They were together from that night on. And then came the letter about the North Beach Peninsula needing doctors. His first thoughts were he already had a practice, a woman who would one day become his wife, a certain peace inside him, but a week later he changed his mind and wrote a letter. . . .

Wesley shivered again. He should eat something, but it was too much trouble and all he wanted was to go to bed and sleep.

The house still had touches of Lucinda. She'd insisted on hanging paintings and making it look like a home. She'd even brought a carpet on the first trip to visit him. Persian in design, it looked out of place with the plain walls of the front room, now serving as a waiting room.

The rug belonged in an elegant parlor, the sort of home where Lucinda had been reared in Portland.

Wesley's thoughts shifted again to Anna. She was determined to be a good nurse. Dedicated in a way Lucinda had never known. Lucinda lived for the moment, whereas Anna lived for eternity. Lucinda had a definite stubbornness about her, but not quite as much as Anna. Her stubbornness reminded him more of determination. Dedication.

His hand touched the worn Bible on the end table, the one gift his mother had left behind—the only thing he had left of her. That and a faded picture.

*God, I don't know You very well, if I ever did. Anna prays to You as if You were a good friend. Her faithfulness amazes me. I find myself dedicated to my profession. I know Anna is dedicated, also. She does not want marriage. Her desire is to be a great nurse. Please put thoughts of Anna from my mind, as I know it will bring nothing but heartache.*

Focused. Wesley remembered Professor James telling him he must stay focused if he was to become a doctor. He would stay focused. He would not think of Anna again—at least not in that way. So far he had acted gruff to hide his feelings.

Wesley padded to the kitchen in search of something. He found bread, butter, and a slice of roast. He gobbled it down and sliced off another chunk of meat.

He sat in the dark, remembering his vow to make certain no more children would ever lose their mother as he had lost his. Callie Fielding flashed into his mind. He hadn't saved her. She'd left two children, just as his mother left two. She was younger, much younger than his mother had been. He had cried when Callie died. If only he could have known what to do. So much for keeping up his end of the bargain.

Then he had nearly lost a second one today. The Clayborne woman. Childbirth. Ordinarily, delivery was easy. But this one could not deliver in the natural way. If it hadn't been for Anna there, assisting him in the surgery, she might have died.

"It's a miracle," Anna had said. "An absolute miracle." This she was telling Peter when he stopped by the boardinghouse. Wesley couldn't help noticing how Peter watched Anna as she spoke. He knew, also, what he was thinking. If only his wife had been spared. But the look that was exchanged between Anna and Peter was more than that. He was certain of it.

Of course. Anna loved Peter. Peter needed her in a way Wesley did not. The children needed a mother. Anna would be a wonderful mother, just as she was a wonderful nurse.

He pushed the plate aside, noting it was nearly ten. After putting his dishes in the sink, he walked to the bedroom and fell across the bed.

*Anna and Peter.* Why hadn't he realized it before now? They would make a beautiful couple. And Peter's prayers would be answered.

Wesley turned off the light, but his mind would not go to sleep. Visions of Lucinda flashed before him. Then Anna's smile. Her laugh. Her eyes serious and ever so blue. Anna who cared for others and Lucinda who cared for no one but herself. There was no comparison between the two, yet he found both had entwined arround his heart and mind like ivy around a tree. What was he to do? How could he stay here? How could he *not* stay?

It was almost daylight before he slipped into sleep.

## nine

July faded into August, and with August Anna found the weather more to her liking. There'd been three weeks in a row without a drop of rain. The path going from the boardinghouse to the beach was dusty and powdery, making her think about Iowa and how she'd liked to trudge barefoot along the paths.

Each Sunday Anna went to the small community church near the boardinghouse. Sometimes she walked, but usually she accepted a ride from Peter Fielding. He came to dinner once a week, sometimes more often. Some Sundays they went swimming at the Crystal Baths. Other times they hiked in the woods, or picnicked in a meadow.

September came and Albert had not yet come to visit, to Anna's keen disappointment. His notes always said he was too busy; the fishing was better than ever, but soon the season would be over and he would need to find work. Then, he planned on a trip to visit Anna.

Pearl wrote on a regular basis. This particular morning, Anna withdrew the last letter from the pink envelope and read its contents again.

*My Dearest Sister Anna,*
*I wish you were here. There are many wonderful things to share with you, to tell you about.*
*Paul is working long hours as a plasterer and so I am alone, but not really. One is never alone*

*when she has God.*

*I fear our Emily is not doing well, but I dare
not say anything to Ben as he has enough to
worry about as is. Please include her in your
prayers.*

Anna read the words again. As if she didn't already
pray for Emily. She prayed for all of her family. She
prayed for Peter, Catherine, and Henry. And, yes, even
Dr. Snow, though she knew he would scoff if she ever
told him this.

She rose, straightened the doily on the table, and carried her cup to the kitchen. Why did she have a problem
with Dr. Snow? Why did she want to be with him when
he clearly did not approve of her? Not that she wasn't a
good nurse, but it was her manner he appeared not to
like. Maybe it was her laugh. Sometimes it slipped out
and she had to put her hand over her mouth to bury it.
She looked in the hall mirror, noticing how much longer
her hair was. It stood out, making her want to use hair oil
as men did. Anything to make it lie flat.

Horses' hooves sounded in the distance and she grabbed
the navy blue straw hat and jammed it down over the can-
tankerous hair. Bessie had found the hat in her closet and
gave it to Anna just yesterday.

Peter came to the door, as he always did. He nodded
when he saw the hat. "New bonnet, right?"

"It's Bessie's."

The children hugged her and soon they arrived at the
church. Anna heard the music before she got down from
the buggy. The words to the song came flowing over her
as she sang the words aloud.

"Constantly abiding—Jesus is mine;
    Constantly abiding—Rapture divine!
He never leaves me lonely—
    Whispers O so kind
Constantly abiding,
    Jesus is mine!"

"How do you know all the words?" Catherine asked, slipping her hand inside Anna's.

"I remember it from when I was in nursing school. The church I attended was huge with a pipe organ and a piano." Yet even as Anna remembered it, she knew she would rather be in this tiny church with her few friends, with the sound of the ocean in the background, than in the big church in the city. This was home. Her home. Peter was looking at her in a different sort of way and Anna hurried on inside, Catherine on one side, Henry on the other.

They went to the front. This way the children seemed less restless. It was as if they knew Pastor Keating could see them, so they sat much more still. Peter slipped into the aisle seat, as always. He looked at Anna and winked.

They opening hymn was another favorite: "Rock of Ages."

"You know that one, too?" Catherine asked as they finished the fourth verse.

"Yes," Anna said. "I know most of them, I suspect."

The door opened and heads turned. Anna gasped. It was the Claybornes. Mrs. Clayborne held her infant daughter as they made their way toward the front.

"A special blessing is in store for us today," Reverend Keating began. "We have the honor and privilege of welcoming one of our new arrivals: Anna Marie Clayborne."

Anna felt her insides tingle as she watched the couple walk up front.

"Anna, would you come and be a witness?" Reverend Keating asked.

Anna walked to the front and took the small baby in her arms. She was so very beautiful with her tiny rose-bud-shaped mouth and a frizz of hair that peeked out from under a white bonnet. The flowing white gown engulfed the tiny body. Anna swallowed with pride. Big brother Edward had a too-large shirt and well-worn trousers. His hair was slicked back, and he looked proud and happy to be standing with his parents and baby sister.

The door opened and Anna looked up to see the familiar tall, broad-shouldered man dressed in black suit and tie. The breath caught in her throat. What was Dr. Snow doing here? He'd never come to church before.

His footsteps approached, as Anna realized he was coming to the front. He stepped up to Mr. Clayborne and shook the man's hand.

Pastor Keating smiled and looked out at the congregation. "Dr. Snow—whom most all of us know—has consented to be this precious one's godparent."

Anna smiled and nodded toward Dr. Snow, but he was looking at the baby in wonderment.

The words were said, prayers offered, and then Reverend Keating said, "I dedicate thee to God, in the name of the Father, the Son, and the Holy Ghost."

Anna's heart swelled with pride. To have a baby named after her was one thing, but to be asked to stand up as a witness was even more wonderful and special. And the Claybornes, who had never come to the church, said they would come again.

The dedication ceremony over, Anna sat next to the children. They were extra quiet. Anna wondered if Dr. Snow would now leave, but the door did not open and she knew he must be sitting with the Clayborn es. Something about his presence had unnerved her more than ever, and she didn't know why.

*Lord,* Anna found herself praying, *I know this isn't the man You would have for me. Why can I not still these feelings then?*

With trembling fingers she opened the hymnal to the closing song.

"Be Thou my Vision, O, Lord of my heart. . ."

Anna's voice sang out clear and true. Yes, she must keep her eye on the vision—her vision. Helping others, being there to assist Dr. Snow when needed.

The service was over and Anna waited for those in front of her to move. Peter got caught talking to Mrs. Farnsworth. Catherine and Henry had run outside to wait. She heard parishioners saying hello to Dr. Snow. Of course he would be greeted, as everybody knew him and respected him highly.

And then he was at her side. "Anna, good morning."

"Good morning, Dr. Snow. How nice to see you here."

"I was asked to come, and so I did."

She glanced up into his eyes and it was as if the world did not exist. Voices hummed in the background, people milling all around her, but Anna saw nothing but Dr. Wesley Snow's face, his dark eyes that held her gaze.

"No emergencies during the night?" she finally asked, for want of something to still her pounding heart. This was ridiculous.

Before he could answer, a voice interrupted. "Dr. Snow!

How wonderful to see you in church. We would love to have you come for dinner, if that's possible."

"Lily. It's good to see you're up and about on that leg."

Lily smiled and clasped his hand. Anna moved past and on up the aisle, the woman's voice penetrating her thoughts. "We do enjoy having company on Sundays."

"Well, I—"

*Go,* Anna was thinking. *Lily Hardin makes a good meal.*

Anna smiled and answered greetings as she headed out the door. The small slip of blue now filled half the sky and she thanked God for the sun, for the warmth, for the wonderful day He had made. A sudden breeze came out of nowhere and lifted her hat.

Anna reached, but couldn't stop it from flying off. And then Peter was there, grabbing it and handing it over.

"To the rescue again," Anna said. "You're always catching my hats."

"I wish I could catch something else—"

Anna turned and asked him to repeat what he'd said, what she thought he'd said.

"Nothing," he said, grabbing Henry and tossing him into the air.

Before Anna could comment, Dr. Snow was at her side. "Had to turn down Miss Lily's dinner invitation since Bessie asked me yesterday to come for the midday meal."

"But this is Sunday."

"I know, but one does not refuse Bessie. Besides, she's making fresh peach pies. How could I possibly stay away from that?" His dark eyes twinkled with a teasing merriment that Anna found disarming.

That was true. Well it would be a full house today as

Peter and the children were staying.

The Clayborns came out then and Anna went over to give the baby one last kiss on the cheek.

"Thank you for asking me to stand up with you."

"It was Dr. Snow's suggestion," Mrs. Clayborne said. "We thought it a good idea, too."

The smell of beef roast filled the boardinghouse as the five entered. Anna knew the roast would be accompanied by slices of onion, whole carrots, and halved potatoes. Too bad Albert wasn't here, as he loved roast and especially peach pie.

Anna left Wesley downstairs talking to another guest who had come in last evening on the train. Slipping into her room, she put the damaged hat on the dresser and patted her hair into place. She would leave her best chambray on, but grabbed a pinafore to wear over it, since she felt led to help in the kitchen.

As Anna started down the stairs, she thought she heard a familiar voice, but it wasn't until she entered the dining room that her heart jumped to her throat. Sitting at the head of the table was her brother Albert!

"Albert! But I thought you couldn't come until November."

"What? And forget my sister's birthday?"

Anna stopped, her face turning red. "Birthday?" Then she remembered. She hadn't thought of it, not once. But Albert had. Twenty-eight. And unmarried.

"This is such a wonderful surprise!"

And then she knew that was why Dr. Snow had turned down Lily's invitation, why Peter had said he and the children would be there.

Bessie came from the kitchen carrying a birthday cake.

"Surprise!" she called out. "I do love surprises."

"And I thought we were having peach pie," Dr. Snow said.

"And so we are," Bessie said.

It was too much. Anna grabbed for the back of the chair and tried hard to bite back the tears. Albert was there, throwing his arms around her. "I got someone to cover for me last night. Came in on the train and you never suspected."

"Bessie said we had a guest, but I never thought—oh, Albert," and she hugged him again harder.

Anna knew her cheeks were still red when the dinner plates had been cleared and it was up to her to cut her cake. Such a day it had been. And Albert had to leave soon to catch the train back so he'd be there for the morning work.

"This has been the most wonderful day ever," Anna said, accepting a small gift from Catherine. It was a picture she'd drawn with the new tablet and paints Anna had given her last week.

There were other gifts, but none as precious as the handmade picture.

After another hug, Albert left to catch his train, Peter left with two very tired children, and Dr. Snow spoke of leaving, too.

"You can have tomorrow off, if you want."

Anna looked into his eyes for a lingering moment. "Thank you, but no, I'd rather come in to work, if that's all right with you."

"Of course."

Long after everyone had left and the house was quiet, Anna sat in her favorite spot and pondered over the day.

It had been a wonderful day, a wonderful surprise, but she felt more confused than ever. Why had Dr. Snow looked at her in that intense way? Why had Peter said what he had in the churchyard? Why was her life suddenly seeming topsy-turvy? Was it possible, could she be falling in love? Yet, she couldn't let it happen. She'd come to be a nurse. Her career meant everything to her. Marriage was not even a consideration. She thought of Joseph. How long since he'd crossed through her thoughts, since she'd looked at his photograph. She knew now that part of her life was over. She was no longer an Iowa girl. She was a woman now, a woman who lived and loved the primitive beauty of the North Beach Peninsula.

As the stars beamed out of a dark sky, Anna thanked God for bringing her here.

# ten

Peter glanced at the profile of the woman he admired, though he knew little about her except that she was happy, energetic, always ready for the occasion. He had done much soul searching last night when sleep wouldn't come.

He missed Callie, her sweet smile, the way she had taken his hand and pulled him close, nestling her head against his chest. Had it really only been a little over a year since her death? Somehow it seemed an eternity. He imagined his hands found her hair, burying them in the soft thickness. It had always been that way—ever since the Johnsons first came to North Beach. The young couple had known at first glance they would be together forever. There never had been anyone else for Peter. . . .

Peter got up and walked out of the bedroom. He didn't see how he could sleep in that empty, cold bed tonight. Thoughts of Callie wouldn't let him rest. He needed someone, yet wondered how he could even consider marrying again. Always, always Callie's face would get in the way. He thought of Anna—how it might be to turn and see her face on the opposite pillow. She would smile or laugh that loud, hearty laugh and then he would remember a soft, tinkling one and—well—he didn't think he could ever love Anna in that special, tender way. Yet he needed her. The children desperately needed a mother, and he must think of them.

Doris Yates, his neighbor on the next farm, cared for

them now—said it was no problem to add two more to her three. Her husband had died at sea three years ago, and it was a struggle eking out a living, but she managed okay. And of course Peter paid her some, but mostly helped out by doing things around the house that only a man could do.

When he'd returned from Portland that last time—after meeting and accompanying Anna—and picked up Catherine and Henry, she'd invited him to come for the next day's evening meal. It seemed he was falling into a pattern, and he didn't want Doris to make anything of it.

Peter added wood to the fire and paced across the front room. It was decision time, but he wasn't ready to make one. Would he ever be?

"Is Anna the one you've sent me?" Peter asked God. He'd never thought of her as beautiful, but there'd been a glow about her as she held little Anna up in front of the church. And later when they'd gone over for the birthday celebration, her eyes were still shining.

He liked being with her. She'd been such a good sport about nearly drowning, then gone clamming and worked right alongside him. It had felt good to have a helpmate again. Callie had loved clamming.

They'd come home late, and Anna had helped clean the clams. She loved everyone and everything. And she believed. That was important to Peter, whose grandfather had been a minister and had encouraged the young Peter in his faith.

The children loved her. He hadn't seen them smile as they did when Anna was around. Surely she loved them. Perhaps not him, but she cared for them. He was positive of that. She might have loved him if it hadn't been for Dr.

Snow. He seemed to turn her head lately. Peter had noticed all right.

"I've prayed for someone, Lord. I need a mother for my kids. I need a wife, though I cannot love her as I loved Callie. Please do not ask that of me."

The fire had died down and it was too late to put another log on. After their afternoon at Bessie's, the children had fallen asleep immediately.

Anna. So spirited. Talkative. Loud. Much louder than his gentle Callie. But she was good with the children and they already adored her. Had she come to North Beach Peninsula to find a husband? Perhaps her job wasn't to nurse the sick and wounded, but to mother Catherine and Henry, to be a wife to him. He needed some sign to know she was the right one.

Peter picked up the oval frame holding Callie's picture. Her eyes seemed to look into his. Her smile was for him alone. They had always loved each other. Cared about each other. It was almost as if they'd signed a pact, promising to belong to no other. And they'd had eight glorious, beautiful years. Until the fever. Sometimes it seemed as if ten years had gone by since he'd felt her arms around him, her mouth raised to his. *Oh, Callie, I love you so. How can I pledge vows to another?*

❧

Wesley Snow had not wanted to leave the boardinghouse. He had not wanted the evening to end. For some reason, he could not keep his eyes off of Anna. Once he had seen Peter watching him. And Bessie. She saw everything, but kept it to herself. Wesley knew he did not need Anna in his life now. After all, he was engaged to Lucinda.

He withdrew the letter he'd received just yesterday.

*My Dear Wesley,*
   *As the time draws near for my trip to the*
*peninsula, I know I can convince you of what you*
*must do. This nonsense has lasted a year now—I*
*gave in to your whim of the heart—now it's your*
*turn to give in to mine. I want us to be married at*
*the huge Presbyterian Church in downtown*
*Portland. It is the place to marry. We can have a*
*most grand and elaborate wedding there.*

Wesley let the letter flutter to the floor as he leaned
back, hands on chest. He didn't want a big wedding. It
wasn't his way of doing things. He wanted to help people. Far better to donate money to the poor people who
had nothing than to waste it on a lavish wedding with so
much food, wine, and flowers.

As for his leaving the peninsula, he could not do it. He
had just won the trust of some of the old-timers. How
could he desert them now? Would someone come to care
for them if he left? He leaned down and picked up the
letter.

   *Darling, I do miss you, you know. We are*
*going to have a wonderful life together, you'll*
*see.*
   *Papa has said we can honeymoon in the*
*Caribbean, if you so choose. I think it's time you*
*got away from the responsibilities of doctoring.*
   *One more thing, darling, there is an Autumn*
*Ball there close to your home. It's held in Long*

*Beach each year. I am bringing a new gown and
dancing slippers and expect you to make sure
you can take off during that time. Let that nurse
take over for you.*

*By the way, Lizzie sent me a picture of her.
She's a homely thing, isn't she? I guess one must
work if she can never hope to marry.*

Wesley wadded the letter into a ball and threw it
toward the fireplace. Imagine. Lucinda thought beauty
was everything. She could not understand the inner
beauty, nor would she probably ever understand.

The embers had died down and he looked at the letter,
knowing it would be ashes by morning. He half expected
Lizzie to come down, asking if he needed a cup of coffee
or something. It was just as well. He'd much rather be
left with his own thoughts.

Wesley closed his eyes and tried to visualize Lucinda,
but for some reason, another face kept getting in the way.
A wonderful, plain face to be sure, but one with a warm
expression and eyes that danced. And most important, was
the laugh that started at the bottom of her toes and worked
all the way up and out, filling the room with its raucous
noise.

*Anna. Oh, Anna, I love you more than I ever thought I
could love anyone or anything. What am I going to do
now? How can I marry Lucinda? How can I tell her no
and make her understand my life is not in Portland, but
here? Here with these people I've grown to love. People
who need me. People I need back.*

## eleven

September ended, and October came with the hint tha[t] winter wasn't far behind. Anna spent her evenings read[-] ing books Emily had sent. There were also books fo[r] Catherine, who was learning to read in school. Often, o[n] Sunday afternoons, Anna would listen to her struggl[e] with new words and encourage her to read and to alway[s] do her best in school. Bessie taught Catherine to cross[-] stitch and she had made several samplers.

"You know what I'm going to do?" Anna said on[e] afternoon. The inspiration had hit when the box of book[s] first arrived.

"No, what?" Bessie asked.

"What we need is a library. Why can't we use one sec[-] tion of the living room here for books? Lots of peopl[e] could use them."

Bessie smiled. "Yes. It's a wonderful idea ye have. I'[ll] put out a plea for people to bring their books when they'v[e] finished them. We'll have the peninsula's first lendin[g] library."

Soon the shelves were full and Bessie asked their neigh[-] bor to build more. Anna had made cards with holders fo[r] each book. The idea caught on and she felt good about it[.] One of the prized possessions was *The Lyric Musi[c] Series—the First Reader.* Bessie seemed to think it ha[d] been used in early schools.

As October drew to a close, Anna knew the beautifu[l]

Lucinda would arrive soon. She looked forward to meeting Dr. Snow's fiancée yet felt fear and trepidation without knowing why.

Thursdays were spent going over the ledger. So many unpaid statements. Never one to press, Dr. Snow accepted a dozen eggs, a slab of ham, vegetables, whatever a patient had an abundance of.

Anna ate the sandwich she'd brought that morning, wishing now for a cup of Bessie's steaming clam chowder, but not daring to leave, lest someone should come.

Perhaps she would travel to Portland on Thanksgiving to spend the holiday with Ben and Emily, Pearl and Paul. Pearl had written recently, excited with the news of a first baby due in June.

The fire bell sounded. Anna froze. The bell meant an emergency. Was it a fire or some medical emergency? Anna prayed for whatever the tragedy might be. She hoped it wasn't a home fire where children might be trapped. Home fires were prevalent, and Anna held her breath, hoping it was only minor.

Minutes later, Anna heard the sound of horses pulling up out front, a voice crying out. "Burn victim! We need help!"

Anna threw open the door and ran out, staring at the small form in the man's arms. She gulped.

"Dr. Snow is on his way. Said you'd know what to do."

The small child couldn't have been more than two years of age. Anna swallowed as the tiny figure was hurried in. Her cries and moans filled the hallway. Anna pulled back the blanket and gasped. It was far worse than she could have imagined. The skin on over half the body was no longer pink, but blackened. The hair was gone and the only way one could tell it was a face was from the two tiny eyes peering out at her. Anna's fingernails dug into her palms.

"Lay her in the examining room at the far end of the hall," she finally commanded. Scrubbing up, she braced herself for this task, the worst she'd ever faced.

The nightgown must come off. And with it would come layers of skin. How could she do it?

"It's okay. You're going to be okay," she soothed, hoping the child could hear her. *O God, give me the strength I need, Keep me calm. Help me to do the right thing. And, please, bring Dr. Snow here quick!*

"How did this happen?" Anna asked one of the firemen standing by.

"House fire up out of Long Beach," the fireman said. "Couldn't reach the mother and another child. She's the only survivor. Father's off working. What a shock he's going to have when he returns."

"Oh, no."

*How horrible,* Anna thought, *to come home to find your home burned to the ground, no belongings left, but most of your loved ones gone.*

"Is someone trying to reach him?"

"Yes, the logging camp's been notified."

Anna started to touch the stockings on the tiny feet, but the child jerked and screamed louder. She fought back another wave of nausea. How could she handle it? If only Dr. Snow were here. . . .

"Found her in the crib—in a back room. Her backside may be okay and the wet diaper gave some protection."

Anna nodded. She'd seen burn patients before, but never one so young. She was just a baby who hadn't even started to live yet, and now it looked as if she might die. Of course, she wasn't the doctor; it could look worse than it was.

Dr. Snow rushed in, filling the room with his knowledge. "Here, Anna, let me see." He gasped, looking away for a long moment. "I'll scrub up, then we must remove the nightgown as slowly as possible. Be prepared. The skin is going to come, too."

They worked together, each looking away, hardly able to stand the sight. "We'll use this salve. It should take away some of the pain."

Anna opened the jar and put huge gobs on the tiny limbs. She felt her head swim and grabbed the edge of the table and held on tight.

Dr. Snow gave her a quick sideways glance. "Anna, go sit. Put your head between your legs and stay for a minute. You look as if you're about to faint. I can't handle two patients just now."

Anna did as she was told. Dr. Snow recognized she was in shock. Though she prepared herself for some of the most gruesome of tasks, one could never be completely prepared. Ten minutes later she reappeared. The child needed constant care. She needed to be turned and given fluids to replace those she'd lost. She could not be left alone. They'd take turns staying with her around the clock.

It was hours later when Dr. Snow told her to leave. "If you can come back after a few hours' sleep, I'd appreciate it. You go now. Bessie is there to talk to. Cry if you must. You can't hold it in."

Anna nodded. "I'll be back."

"Anna?" He stepped out into the hall.

She turned and something about the expression on his worn face made her heart leap. "Yes?"

His face returned to the usual mask. "She may not make it. You must prepare yourself for that possibility."

"O God, please, no," Anna prayed. Covering her mouth with her hands, she sat in the nearest chair.

႙

All was quiet when Anna arrived at the boardinghouse. A note was on the table. "Scones in the bread box; pie in the pie keeper."

Anna couldn't eat. All she wanted to do was forget the baby fighting for her life—the smell of burning flesh—the way it was not only in her uniform, but saturated in her hair, her cap, her nostrils. She knew as she threw the uniform in a heap in the corner of her bedroom, that the smell would not leave her soon.

Four hours later, after a fitful sleep, Anna rose and fumbled with the buttons of her clean uniform. It was black and cold outside, as she headed back to the hospital, not realizing she'd even arrived until Ned trotted up to the side. She hurried inside, and the smell of coffee revived her. Lizzie thrust a cup into her hands. "Here. Drink this before going in there."

So the child still lived. Her uneven breathing filled the room as Anna came, standing over the small form. Dr. Snow glanced up, as if just realizing she'd come and his eyes filled with relief. "Did you sleep?"

Anna nodded. "As well as could be expected under the circumstances."

He raised red-rimmed eyes to her. "She's still with us," he murmured.

"I see that. It's your turn to go get rest now."

He tried to straighten up. "Yes, you're right. I'll be upstairs if you need me." He ran a hand through his disheveled hair. "Let me know if her condition worsens."

"I will."

It was later that Lizzie reminded Anna of Lucinda's impending arrival.

"And the Autumn Ball is the next day, is that right?"

Lizzie nodded. "Heaven help us if Dr. Snow should decide not to go."

Anna couldn't think of fancy balls now as she forced fluids into the tiny mouth. The little girl moaned as she tossed and turned. Anna prayed that the pain would lessen. So tiny to endure such suffering. If only she could understand why these things happened. Would she live? And if she did, what would she have to live for? With a disfigured face and body, she would never be normal, never be like others. She'd be ridiculed and laughed at, yet Anna must pray for her recovery. The oath she'd taken said she would do everything in her power to help the sick, to administer to their needs and she could do nothing less now.

Anna sat in the chair beside the bed. In a few minutes she'd apply more salve. She hummed a tune and the eyes fluttered open. "I love you, Rebecca," she whispered. She had to turn away, to keep the child from seeing her tears. The first twenty-four hours were crucial. Would Rebecca live to see tomorrow?

# twelve

Lucinda Mae Lawson boarded the *T.J. Potter* at the Portland docks that November morning. Dressed in her best purple damask with full skirt and gathered waist she clutched her latest hat, a wide-brimmed affair with real ostrich feathers. Her gloves matched. Heads turned her way as she climbed aboard the sternwheeler that traveled from Portland to Astoria twice each day. This particular day she would go on the Washington side to Megler Landing, and then board the Clamshell Railroad to her destination in Seaview.

Soon she would be alone, having refused the accompaniment of her mother or best friend Mary Dugan.

"I must learn to do things for myself," had been her answer, and as always Lucinda had her way after much spirited arguing and pouting. The pouting—staying in her room one entire day—had unnerved her father so much he'd said, "I give in! What can possibly happen?" The one request was that she had a place to stay; hence a room rented in advance—the best room, of course—at Bessie McGruder's Boarding House in Seaview.

"Save your pretty frocks for when you arrive and Wesley takes you dancing or partying," Mrs. Lawson had said yesterday, not agreeing with Lucinda's choice of traveling attire.

"Mama, I must look my best whether traveling or not," she proclaimed.

Now as Lucinda boarded, she waved good-bye. Her purpose was twofold. Not only would she be there to attend the Autumn Ball; she would convince Wesley Snow it was time to return to Portland; time to plan for their summer wedding. Surely he had gotten this place out of his system by now. She had waited a year while he played country doctor to the people on the North Beach Peninsula. She'd been more than patient.

Lucinda reminded herself that she did not fall for Dr. Wesley Snow because he was handsome, though he was in a rugged sort of way, but because of the prestige that would follow being married to a doctor. Such things were extremely important to her. Besides, it was time she married before tongues began to wag, saying she was an old maid. Twenty-two was not old, but she had waited long enough to receive the inheritance from Grandfather Lawson. His will stipulated she must be married before she received the legacy.

At last the boat was on its way. An hour later, Lucinda sighed, already more than a little weary from her trip, and they were only halfway down the Columbia River. It would be late before she arrived at her destination.

Two trunks had been carefully packed. The new gown—a rich blue satin with puffed sleeves—and new shoes, gloves, and stockings lay in one. Lucinda could hardly wait to show off at this annual dance. Surely Wesley would realize how fortunate he was to have her at his side.

She'd wanted to stay at his home; after all their old cook Lizzie Myles was there to chaperone, but her mother put her foot down. "It is not proper, Lucinda, and I will not hear of your staying in the same home as your fiancé—not even if there were five chaperones. The boardinghouse it will be."

At last they arrived at Megler Landing and soon Lucinda was helped to board the evening train heading west.

"Goodness," she exclaimed to the passenger across the aisle. "I always forget how dusty and dirty these trains are."

"Yes, dusty it is," came the reply. The woman dressed in serviceable gray bombazine looked common. Plain. Something like that nurse who had come to work with Wesley a few months ago.

Lucinda turned and stared out the window. Undoubtedly she would meet her at the boardinghouse, as she lived there. And of course there would be that weird lady who ran the place. Bessie with the strange way of saying *ye* for "you."

Lucinda held her left, gloved hand to the window. The ring made a bump in the fabric. Her engagement ring. At first she'd hoped to marry by Christmas, but Wesley hadn't been willing to give up this inane idea to work in such a primitive spot. She could never live here. If she'd had any doubts, any reconsiderations, all had been dashed as she made this trip west, again. How Wesley could enjoy this remote area, why he hadn't wanted to stay in Portland and continue on with the practice, caused her much consternation. Should she marry such an insensitive man?

"My new dress shall need to be cleaned immediately after I arrive," Lucinda said, turning to look at the woman across the aisle.

"One shouldn't wear her best," the woman replied then. "Are you going far?"

Lucinda looked at her, noticing the smudge on her face. Her figure was full, her hair unkempt. "Yes. I have come to see my husband-to-be."

"Oh. And who might that be?"

"Dr. Wesley Snow. Perhaps you know him?"

"Dr. Snow?" The woman's eyes lit up. "Why Dr. Snow saved my husband's life! It was just last month! Oh, my goodness, my golly, and to think you are to be his wife and all."

Lucinda straightened her shoulders and drew back. "I realize that is what my intended does best," and then the words slipped from her mouth before she could stop them. "If he tended to my desires, my dreams half as well, I wouldn't be coming here now with an ultimatum."

"Ultimatum?" The woman looked puzzled.

Lucinda, deciding she'd said more than enough, turned away and stared out the window again. All she could see was the lapping waters of the Columbia River and the fish seining camps, the horses pulling the heavy nets. The train chugged west and stopped suddenly. The lady descended at a place called Pt. Ellice. "Oh, please thank Dr. Snow for me again for saving my Ralph's life."

And then she was gone and the train started up again, making its clanging, horrible noise. Lucinda withdrew a handkerchief from her purse and covered her mouth, hoping she didn't have soot in her hair, yet knowing she probably did.

Lucinda's mission would not be easy, but she was good at persuading people to do what she wanted. There were wedding preparations and parties to attend. Surely another doctor, one more suited to this place, could be found.

Lucinda covered her nose again as soot floated through the air in the travel car. There were several stops yet before she'd reach her destination.

She wasn't looking forward to having Bessie pry, or coming face to face with that short-haired, homely nurse. No wonder the poor woman had taken up nursing. Women chose careers when they knew they probably wouldn't marry. And she was old—at least as old as Wesley. But she was a good nurse. Wesley had mentioned it more than once.

The train stopped again and a cow bawled. With the windows open, Lucinda heard the sound and caught the smell. Animals rode two cars back—whatever people brought with them. So quaint, this place. Lucinda would never become used to it. Already she was pining for Portland and its elegance, the party she would miss tomorrow evening. The dance here better be a fancy one. Surely it would be. Even country people must dress up at times.

With a sigh, Lucinda leaned back and closed her eyes.

❧

The young boy who tended the horses met the train that evening. Bessie was expecting Lucinda and had reserved the fanciest room she had. It was on the top floor—across from Anna's.

The groom remembered Lucinda. She'd given him a nickel when he'd brought her trunk to Bessie's the last time.

She signaled him now. "I need help. You do live over yonder in that boardinghouse, is that not correct?"

"Yes, ma'am." He bowed slightly.

"I have two large trunks. I'll need you to take them to

the boardinghouse and on up to my room."

"Yes, ma'am, I can do that."

Bessie had the room aired out and sent the lad up with the trunks. He had to make two trips, so Lucinda gave him two nickels. His eyes lit up as he pocketed the coins. "Thank you, ma'am."

"Come," Bessie said. "Ye must be tired. Ye can have tea with me. Anna is not here yet, but I expect her soon."

"I want to see Wesley."

"Perhaps ye should wait until morning. There's a little girl fighting for her life."

Lucinda's eyes narrowed. "He knew I was coming."

"Yes, he did." Bessie poured tea into a delicate china cup.

Lucinda removed her gloves and hat. "I am a fright from that long, horrendous trip."

"A bath can be drawn for you."

Lucinda nodded. "That will be most necessary. After I have my tea."

After the bath and a change of clothes, Lucinda demanded to be driven to town to see her fiancé.

"Now?" Bessie asked. "It's terribly late."

Lucinda ignored her. "I assume the young man who helped me before can assist me."

Bessie assured her that was possible.

"I simply cannot go to the ball tomorrow night looking like this. Do you have a hairdresser on the premises?"

Bessie'd never had such a request. "There is one in Long Beach. I'm sure they can accommodate ye."

Lucinda sighed. "I suppose that will have to do."

"If ye are ready to go now, Miss Lawson, I'll call my groom. He'll be happy to take ye into town."

Lucinda wore a calico that had been beautiful once. It was wrinkled and she considered having it pressed, but decided time was wasting. She must go see Wesley now. The sooner the better.

❧

Anna sat with Rebecca. It had been twenty-four hours and then some. The child clung to life.

Anna now waited for Dr. Snow to wake up from his rest. She must have dozed off because suddenly she heard a shrill voice. It filled the entire first floor of the infirmary.

"You didn't even come to meet me on the day I arrive!" the voice shrieked.

Anna trembled. Was it Lucinda? Dr. Snow's fiancée? But why would she come here? Wouldn't it have been better to wait at the boardinghouse?

Anna closed the door, but the voices grew louder.

"I cannot attend the ball, tomorrow, Lucinda. I'm sorry, but I can't get away. I have a burn patient who needs—"

"The patients always come first."

"I took an oath—"

"And you also took an oath when we became betrothed. All I want is two hours of your time. Is that asking too much?"

Anna remembered Lizzie's words from the day before. It looked as if her prediction would come true, but she could stay, watch over the patient so Dr. Snow could attend the dance. She went down the hall.

"Dr. Snow, I can stay with Rebecca—"

"See?" Lucinda said. "I knew someone could relieve you."

He turned and held up his hand. "No. I cannot leave

someone so critical—"

"She's a capable person," Lucinda broke in. "Let her take care of the little girl and come with me."

He looked at Anna again, then back at Lucinda. "No. I cannot, Lucinda. We can talk about this later."

"I won't be here later," Lucinda said. Even in the wrinkled calico, she looked exquisite. "I fully intend to be on the train that leaves Sunday."

"Very well. There's nothing I can do to stop you. We both know that."

"We're not talking about stopping," Lucinda said. "Nothing can make me stay in this place. Absolutely *nothing.*"

"That's too bad," he said, turning his back. "You do what you must, Lucinda, just as I do what I must. Now I have a patient I must check and a nurse to relieve. Anna's been here way too many hours." He started off down the hall.

Lucinda gasped and hurried after him. "Not before I have my say!"

He paused and faced the woman he thought he loved at one time. "Go ahead. I'm listening."

"This is an ultimatum, Dr. Wesley Snow. If you can't take me to the Autumn Ball, then we're through." Her mouth had drawn up into a pout. "I understand that you must care for your patients, Wesley. This is fine, but you can go back to your old office with Robert in East Portland. I cannot, I *will not* stay here. You have a month to decide. Surely they can find a doctor to take your place by then." She walked across the waiting room. "Either you come back to Portland then, or our marriage will be called off."

He stared at the woman before him. She was diminutive, a beauty dressed in calico, a large-brimmed hat with ribbons and lace. Her blond curls framed a heart-shaped face and he realized how beautiful she was. But her beauty was only skin deep.

*Leave in one month, indeed!*

Wesley never had liked threats, whether they came from his fiancée or someone else. Something recoiled inside him. He didn't do well with ultimatums. How dare Lucinda tell him what he could or couldn't do? Didn't she understand even a whit of what had brought him here—why he felt he must stay? Had his schooling meant nothing? Did she not understand a man must follow his heart, do what had to be done, what he felt led to do?

Lucinda would have her way. She cared for nobody but herself. He was born to serve, she to be served. It hadn't mattered in the beginning, but it did now. No. He would not be forced to return to Portland to practice. He liked it here. He was needed here. It would be a lonely life, perhaps, yet he knew it could never be so when there were people who needed treatment. People who brought him fresh fish, crabs, clams, and oysters. People who looked out for his needs as well as he did for theirs.

He pushed her words aside, the ones that stipulated what he must do. She stood waiting, eyes still blazing.

"I hope you will be very happy, Miss Lucinda Mae Lawson," he said aloud.

"Oh!" A sound of something hitting the floor, then the door banged once. It opened again as her voice rang out: "I don't want the ring anyway. It was just a cheap thing to begin with!"

Anna held her breath. She hadn't wanted to hear any of

the conversation. Such things should be private, but with Lucinda she wondered if any matter was private. Lizzie Myles came out of the kitchen, wringing her hands. "That Miss Lucinda does have a temper!"

"Yes, well, I believe she may be leaving." Dr. Snow appeared in the doorway. He turned to Anna. "I'm sorry you had to hear this. You, too, Lizzie."

" 'Tisn't the first time I've been parley to Miss Lucinda's wiles, and I'm sure it won't be the last."

"Will she return to Portland?" Anna asked.

"Oh, I'm sure she will. After she creates another scene." He waved his hand. "You go on home now. You look exhausted."

Anna thought he did, too, but she didn't say it. Something made her want to reach up and press fingertips to the lines on his brow. The thought jolted her as she turned away suddenly, looked at Rebecca once more, then hurried out the door.

After Anna left, Wesley Snow thought, again, about Lucinda's display of temper. If he didn't attend the dance, she would leave the peninsula and never return. Somehow a sense of relief filled him at the prospect.

He sighed as he thought of Anna. Things had run smoother since her arrival. She was a stubborn thing, and maybe she was not beautiful like Lucinda, but she knew her work and something drove her from inside. Sort of the same as he felt. He could tell by the concerned look in her eyes, the frown on her face. She worried about each and every one that walked through the door. She was here to take care of that cut, remove the sliver or fish hook.

She was dedicated. He could think of no better word to

describe Anna Galloway. Yet, there was the situation with Peter Fielding.

Should she decide to marry—and he had a feeling that Peter would ask her soon—Wesley would lose her. Peter needed a mother for his children, a wife for his bed. He knew Anna loved them. She loved everyone. *Every-one?* A sudden warmth rippled through him. Strange, but he had never thought of it quite like that.

Anna probably cared for him, just as she did the many patients. Yes, hers was a caring heart.

He walked back to the patient's room and stared at the small child, actually no more than a baby. How could God make this tiny one suffer? How could he believe in a God who allowed such things to happen?

Yet he found himself praying, uttering words he hadn't spoken since he'd sat at his mother's bedside. "God, please ease her suffering. Please, if there is any justice in this world. . ."

## thirteen

As screams of anger, then sobs filled the house, Anna mulled it over, finally deciding to do something about Lucinda. Maybe she could explain why tending to sick people would always come before the desires of the heart. She knew Dr. Snow to be a wonderful, considerate person who would not hurt the woman he loved just to be cruel. He had looked forward to the dance; he had told Anna himself.

Anna found her lying across the bed, sobbing as if her heart would break. "Lucinda." She touched the young woman's shoulder. Lucinda flinched, then bolted up.

"What are you doing in my room? Can't a person have privacy around here?"

Anna swallowed hard. "The door was open. I thought perhaps I could help."

"You've helped enough already!" The cheeks were wet, the eyes now snapping. "I daresay you're the reason Wesley is staying here—"

Anna stepped back, her hand going to her throat. This could not be true. What was Lucinda talking about? No, it wasn't possible. Lucinda was distraught and was the type to strike at anyone who got in her way.

"I can bring you a cup of tea, if you like."

Lucinda shook her head, the curls bouncing. "I do not want any tea and I do not want you to patronize me."

Anna stepped back. "I'm only trying to help."

"Oh, you nurses and doctors are all alike. You think you can solve the problems of the world by bringing someone a cup of tea, by holding her hand, mopping the perspiration off her brow."

At that word, she reached for a lace handkerchief and wiped her forehead. "I prefer not discussing it with you. The only thing for me to do—" she got up and opened the smaller trunk, "is to pack my things and go back to Portland where I belong."

"I wish you would change your mind," Anna said. "The North Beach Peninsula is a lovely place. It grows on you."

"I hate it here!" The voice rose shrilly. "And I especially hate people like you. So sanctimonious. Always so sweet and right. You have people eating out of your hand. I've never been that way and I'm not about to start now!"

Anna stepped backwards as if expecting to get struck. She said nothing.

"You can stay here. Wesley can stay here, but I'm going back to Portland where my kind of people are."

"The doctor loves you very much—"

"And how would you know that?" She spun around and met Anna's steady gaze. "I suppose Wesley confides in you. Isn't that what doctors do with their nurses?"

"I—didn't mean to imply—"

"Well, if he prefers plain to beauty, then he's found the perfect mate in you."

Anna gasped as the words soaked in. "I suppose beauty does matter to most men. And perhaps that's why I never planned to marry, but chose a career instead."

"Don't make it sound any better," Lucinda said. "I said what I meant and meant what I said. Don't try to talk me out of it. If Wesley wants you, he can very well have you!"

Anna left the room without another word.

Lucinda threw clothes into the trunk. She had not wanted to talk to Anna with the smoldering eyes. She made her feel uncomfortable. How dare she think she could tell her how to feel? To act? As if it was any of her business.

She, Lucinda, was somebody. She wasn't a homely nurse from the state of Iowa. Lucinda's great-grandfather had come on a wagon train west; had settled in Salem, a community south of Portland. Later his son, Lucinda's father, moved to Portland, opening up one of the first ladies' shoe stores. Everyone knew the Lawson name.

Lucinda wouldn't be here now if it hadn't been for the stupid will. She didn't even want to marry, not just yet.

Voices came up the back stairs. Lucinda closed her door. She hated boardinghouses where everyone knew everyone else's business.

Anna slipped down the stairs, wondering if everyone had heard. Lucinda's words stung. Though she knew them to be true, they still hurt. Of course she wasn't beautiful. Anyone could see that. Freckles. Shoulders too broad. Mouth too small and just a thin line. What was it Mama had said once? "It's as if the bottom lip had disappeared."

Anna no longer had long tresses to make her look feminine. All men loved long hair—so she'd been told—but short hair was much more practical. She would ignore Lucinda's rantings. Lucinda was hurt. People said things when they hurt inside. She didn't want to go home, or face people saying she had lost the good doctor, the marriage had been called off.

Slipping into the kitchen, Anna moved the teakettle over to the heat of the stove. She needed a cup of tea while she sorted through her thoughts. If Mama was here to talk to, or Pearl—yes Pearl understood about the plain part. She was even taller than Anna, with broader shoulders, but Paul loved her anyway. And Clara in Connecticut. Anna wondered if she'd ever see her sister again. She was the tallest of all, at least six foot in stocking feet.

Anna walked to the window and looked out at the whitecaps. She loved watching the ocean—all-powerful, yet soothing. She wished that Lucinda could find one thing she liked about the peninsula. It really wouldn't be that difficult, but Lucinda made things difficult. It was like Mama's saying: "You can lead a horse to water, but you can't make him drink." Or, "Pretty is as pretty does."

She clasped her hands and thought again about Rebecca. So young to be burned, and not understanding why it hurt so much. Fires were such hazards. Why weren't people more careful?

Anna sipped her tea. A sound of thumping on the main stairwell startled her. It was Lucinda dragging the smaller of the trunks down the steps, thumping at each one. It never occurred to her that others were asleep. Anna thought about helping, but the less she saw of Miss Lucinda Mae Lawson, the better off she'd be.

The voice at her elbow commanded her to turn to face the red-streaked face. "I hope you and Wesley will be very happy together."

Anna shook her head. "If I marry, Lucinda, I can no longer be a nurse and nursing is my career. It's what I want to do with my life." She hesitated for a moment. "Perhaps if you understood that, you'd know why Dr.

Snow has to be a doctor. It's a definite calling."

"Calling!" Lucinda snorted. "He can feel led to treat patients in Portland as well as here!"

Anna put the cup back in the saucer. "Perhaps, but he wants to be needed and this place would then have no doctor. Please, can't you understand?"

"No! Never!"

Bessie appeared around the corner. "I have some lovely scones if ye would like one with a cup of tea."

"When does the train come?" Lucinda asked, ignoring Bessie's offer. "I plan to be on the very next one heading east."

Bessie scowled. "At this hour? Go on to bed. Ye can catch the first one tomorrow. There's nothing tonight."

"See? That's what I mean. You can't depend on anything around here!" Her eyes blazed.

"I'll pack ye a lunch to take. That should help some."

"I don't want to spend one more night here, nor do I want to see Wesley again!"

"I could find an escort to the dance, if ye'd like. Especially since you brought your best taffeta dress and black patent leathers."

Lucinda whirled, her calico flouncing out around her. "I would not wish to go to a dance with someone I did not know, and especially not someone from here. He would probably wear overalls!"

"I see this discussion is going nowhere," Anna said then.

She excused herself and slipped out the door, after grabbing a jacket from the hook on the glassed-in porch. It was late, but a full moon made it light. She needed to go walk on the beach, feel the sand under her sturdy shoes, hear the waves even better, taste the salt spray on her face. It was the best place where she could talk to God.

Tying a woolen scarf around her hair to hold off the wind, Anna tore off across the dirt road and ran toward the water.

There were things she must sort out in her mind. Were her feelings toward Wesley Snow more than just admiration? Surely not. She thought of that first day when he'd stopped at the boardinghouse for lunch. How much Bessie liked him and how well everyone thought of him. It became more apparent as she worked with him, went to homes to tend to broken bones, burns, raging fevers, women having babies, that all loved him. This was where he belonged. Why couldn't Lucinda understand that? Why couldn't she be happy that he was doing what God had called him to do?

Everything seemed to hinge on the dance. Anna closed her eyes and thought what it might be like to attend the dance. She had gone to few dances in her life, but none since she'd become a young woman. No, come to think of it, there was one in Iowa City, one Saturday night when she was in nurse's training. She hadn't danced with anyone, but enjoyed watching the others whirling out on the floor, the beautiful colors blending together as they danced from one end to the other. She wondered suddenly what it might be like to dance in Peter's arms. Or Dr. Snow. She trembled at the thought of Dr. Snow. It was laughable. She only thought of him now since Lucinda had put the thought into her head. She might dream about him all she wanted, but he would never think of her in any way except as a nurse. And a good nurse at that. Hadn't he said so more than once?

Deep in thought, Anna was unaware of a sneaker wave and soon her shoes were full of water.

"Oh! I will never remember to watch the waves," she said aloud. "One cannot take her eyes off the waves." Oh, well, what was a bit of water in one's shoes? She moved up on the sand further and it was as if someone was watching her. She knew, without looking, it was Lucinda. Lucinda already thought she was strange. She no doubt thought it weird anyone would walk on the beach at night, and get caught by a wave.

Cold now, with her stockings full of water and sand, Anna walked back to the boardinghouse. She'd slip past Bessie, and up to her room to change, but Bessie sat in the doorway, arms crossed. "I see ye been wading with your shoes on again!" The smile was impish.

"Yes, some of us never learn, do we?"

"Aye. I know how ye think things over. Ye get all caught up in the problems of the world and the problems of other people." She handed Anna a towel and took her coat and scarf. "Her Royal Highness has gone to bed, against her better judgment. She'll be up bright and early, or so she said."

"Lucinda is not the type to rise early," Anna said, not wanting to think about her anymore. "Think I'll go to bed, too."

Anna thought of Dr. Snow again as she tiptoed up the stairs, feeling the wet, hearing the squishy sound of each step. Why had Lucinda said such things? Now his face kept flashing through her mind.

She slipped into bed, too exhausted to read Scripture, or say her prayers. She must go early tomorrow to take care of Rebecca.

ะ

Little Rebecca Sims died Saturday afternoon, at the precise time Lucinda boarded the train. Died with Dr. Snow at her side, before Anna came on duty again. He cried only a moment before pulling the sheet up over the burned face. Her father hadn't arrived in time to see her, but perhaps it was just as well. This child was not the one he'd left behind. Dr. Snow thanked God for His ultimate mercy. They'd done all they could, but it hadn't been enough. He hoped that someday there would be a way to help burn victims more. Or, better yet, perhaps fires could be prevented. There had to be some answers. There just had to be.

# fourteen

Days slipped into weeks and with that came changes. Anna did not go to Portland for Thanksgiving and soon it looked as if she wouldn't be going at Christmas. There was too much to do, with too little time to do it. A bad strain of flu had hit the peninsula, and even Anna came down with the debilitating symptoms. After the fever and achiness were gone, Anna was exhausted. Dr. Snow sent her home on two consecutive days.

"We don't want to give this to any of the patients."

She knew he was right, but had thoroughly expected to feel better. Working was what she needed to help her escape the lethargy. She was tired of the confining walls of her bedroom, the downstairs parlor. Bessie and the other boarders were sick, but nobody as sick as she.

"She just let herself get run down with too much work and not enough play," was Bessie's answer.

"That is true," Dr. Snow nodded in agreement.

It was lunchtime and Anna was sitting in a far corner of the living room, gazing out at the gray sky. The day looked the way she felt. Still, she was perturbed that they were talking about her, almost as if she were a child who needed reprimanding.

Anna curled up and fell asleep, listening to the chatter of voices in the background. She wakened as a shadow crossed in front of her. Dr. Snow leaned down, pressing his mouth against her forehead. She jumped.

"Sorry." He backed off. "Just wanted to see if the fever was still there."

Their eyes met, and Anna tried to smile.

"I need you back at work, but I need you to get completely well so very much more."

He turned and walked away before she could answer.

Dr. Snow never did contract the flu, and Anna fully recovered two weeks before Christmas.

"Oh, Bessie!" she cried coming down the stairs one morning. "It's as if I turned over a page in one of my books. I'm starting a new chapter. I feel *good*." She stretched, then hugged the older lady close. "What would I have done without your chicken soup and endless pots of tea?"

"And prayers," Bessie added.

"Yes, and prayers."

"Did ye know the good doctor climbed the stairs every day, looking in on ye?"

Anna's face flushed. "No. I didn't."

"He was mighty worried about ye. Think he even said some prayers, himself."

Anna finished her second cup of coffee and rose to go. "I'm ready to go back now. How I've missed being out of the middle of things."

"There was a shipwreck a week ago, and ye didn't even know it—ye were still sleeping a lot. No victims this time. Just a crabber that came in too close and got stuck. Boat demolished when high winds came."

"Oh, no." Anna hated it that Dr. Snow'd had to tend to all the little details—bringing in food—changing linens—in her absence.

"He asked Lizzie to help."

Anna returned to work with renewed vigor. She'd never

felt better, or more energetic. Peter and the children stopped by on Sunday and they made the usual trek to church.

"And you never got the flu?" Anna asked.

Peter shrugged. "Strong constitution, I guess."

"We got sick!" Catherine said. "I yukked up in the kitchen!"

"Me, too," said Henry, not to be outdone by his sister.

It was good to be back and Anna sang the hymns with gusto. Her voice rang out with "Blessed Assurance, Jesus Is Mine."

"I was worried about you," Peter offered on the drive back to the boardinghouse. They'd decided against going anywhere because Anna didn't want to overdo.

Bessie had fixed a meal to beat all. Glazed ham, corn fritters, her famous fruit salad, with dried-apple pie to top it off.

Later the children, Anna, and Peter went to the middle floor and played checkers and dominos.

"You look happy today," Peter commented after Henry had fallen asleep on the small settee.

"I am, Peter. I'm very happy and feel so blessed."

His hand touched hers. "I don't suppose you've been thinking about me—about us. Maybe missing us a little?"

Anna smiled. She was so very fond of Peter, Catherine, and Henry, but did her feelings for him go deeper? How did one know for sure?

"I'm glad you're part of my life," she finally answered.

He nodded. "I guess that's what I'm a thinking, too."

Christmas was approaching fast, and Bessie said it would be the best one ever. "I'm going to make this old place shine!"

Anna helped Bessie decorate the downstairs. They set up a tree—a fine, bushy beach pine, which Catherine and Henry helped decorate with paper chains while she and Cora strung popcorn and cranberries. Anna was forever nibbling on the popcorn, but the cranberries were tart and not to her liking.

Emily sent more books—coloring books—crayons for the children, and decorations for the tree. They were shiny glass balls with silver centers. She'd packed them well, and not one was broken. Everyone thought they were beautiful.

Anna had tried to knit in the evenings, but she wasn't like her mother. Knitting was far from enjoyable. She'd get busy talking and have to rip out several rows. She finally gave up and bought gifts from the mercantile. Peppermint sticks for Ben, chocolates for Emily, who must miss the confections since she no longer worked at the candy factory. Chocolates, also, for family friends Kate and Pastor Luke. A bright red shirt for Clifford, a knitted sweater Cora had made, for baby Hazel, who had arrived December 1. She gave both Peter and Dr. Snow pairs of socks she had knitted year before last. Maybe they wouldn't notice that one sock had an extra row. Bessie was the problem. What to give to her? At last she chose a new lace tablecloth for the small round table in the parlor.

On Sunday Bessie asked Peter to help her loop green garlands across the high ceiling in the parlor and a string of lights along the front windows. "I had these sent over from Astoria," she explained.

There was the baking of fruit cakes, sugar and ginger cookies, date bars, and a double batch of shortbread, a favorite from Bessie's native Scotland.

"The pies will be made the day before Christmas," Bessie proclaimed. "We're having a full house, as I've invited everyone I know!"

"Not everyone!" Cora exclaimed. "Surely not everyone."

Bessie nodded. "Yes. Guess ye don't know I had extra leaves for the table. I want no one to go without a good home-cooked meal. The menu includes turkey, ham, lots of sweet and white potatoes. Corn and peas. And Sally Lunn bread because that's what Dr. Snow requested."

Anna thought about what she liked. Mama had always made cut-out sugar cookies, so she asked if Catherine might not help her in the kitchen. After they were baked, Henry could help decorate them. It would be a festive holiday.

"What about Albert?" Anna asked then. "Maybe he can come."

"Already done." Bessie smiled as if she knew a deep, dark secret.

"What is it? Tell me, please tell me," Anna implored.

"He's bringing a lady friend, that's what."

Christmas Eve was spent around the fireplace while Anna read the story about Jesus' birth. Bessie offered prayers, then all had hot, spiced tea and lemon cake.

Christmas morning, which Anna had looked forward to for weeks, dawned cold, gray, and foggier than usual. As she bustled around, helping Bessie set the table, bells rang out.

"Oh, no, not today!" Bessie cried. "What's going on?"

"It's the bell at our church," Peter said.

"Aren't they pretty sounding, Papa?" Catherine asked, her eyes shining.

"Yes," agreed Anna. "Like bells of old, proclaiming our dear Savior's birth."

A sudden knock sounded and Henry ran to open the door. When he saw the big man standing there, he stepped aside.

"Hello! Merry Christmas!"

"Albert! You made it!" Anna cried, running to embrace her brother. She looked perplexed. "Where's your lady friend?"

Albert laughed. "She couldn't make it. But, never mind. Look what I brought!" He set the box down. "Go ahead. Open it," he said to Henry.

Henry looked at his father, then back at Albert. "Go ahead," Peter said. "It's all right."

Henry bent down and tugged at the top. Albert leaned over. "Here. I'll help."

"Oranges!" Catherine said, after peering inside. "Oh, Papa, it's oranges!"

"Oranges?" Bessie exclaimed. "We haven't had oranges for so long. Nearly forgot what they tasted like. What a splendid gift."

Soon guests began arriving, and just before Dr. Snow came, Anna slipped upstairs to change into the sea-green taffeta. Her maid of honor gown. She loved it. Pressing down the folds, she turned sidewise to stare into the mirror. A comb in her hair, and she was ready for the banquet. Christmas Day. Such a joyous occasion, but it was what they were celebrating that meant more than anything.

Dr. Snow, dressed in dark suit and white shirt, looked handsome and Anna smiled as their eyes met.

After all guests sat, Bessie, Anna, and Delia began

bringing the food in. Bessie asked Peter to give thanks for this most blessed of all days, for the bounty of food, but especially for friends and family.

# fifteen

It was January 1913. Woodrow Wilson had been elected president, but would not be inaugurated until March. At the boardinghouse things had been quiet due to bad weather. Dr. Snow and Anna had kept busy tending to colds and broken bones.

On Saturday morning Anna was helping Bessie in the kitchen when the wire came.

"Imagine Miss Lucinda Lawson sending Dr. Snow a message here," Bessie said. "She has more chutzpa than anyone I've met." She looked up from the dough she had rolled out. "Hand me a knife, will ye?"

"Is he going to change his mind? About going back to Portland?" Anna asked.

"How should I know, child? I don't know everything that happens around here."

"Not everything, but pretty close," a voice said from the doorway. It was Gloria, one of the boarders who had moved in last week.

Bessie began cutting the dough. "Aye, I know a lot that goes on, but I never, ever gossip about people."

Anna wished she'd never asked now. Bessie turned to put the two huge pans of rolls in the waiting oven and washed her hands. "Why don't ye two go out on the beach. It's the nicest day we've had in a month of Sundays."

"I think a walk would rid my head of cobwebs and stir some new blood in my brain," Anna said.

"You are so funny," Gloria said. "I like talking to you because you make me think about things."

Gloria wore a green and white gingham and a straw hat that no way covered her blond curls. She was young, unmarried, and was shy around everyone else.

"You're fun to be with because you are a good listener," Anna answered.

Gloria and Anna walked across the road to the beach. They had taken along a small bag with apples and two of Bessie's oatmeal cookies. They found a nice spot and sat on the sand, knees tucked under them. The weather was almost hot, to Anna's delight.

"Do you really like nursing?" Gloria asked.

Anna nodded. "I hope to do it the rest of my life."

"And never marry?"

"And never marry." She wanted to tell Gloria about Joseph and how she had plans to give up her nursing when they married, but Gloria was onto another subject.

"I think it's a mistake to ignore that young man who comes around."

"Young man?" Anna sat up straighter. "Do you mean Peter?"

"He has two children. Bessie spoke with him on the sunporch yesterday." Gloria scooped sand into her hand, then let it sift through her fingers. "I wouldn't mind if he came calling on me. I think he's utterly handsome!" She smiled impishly.

Anna supposed Peter was handsome with that sandy hair and his dark eyes.

"I must go back," Gloria said then. "I burn real easy." She jumped up, brushing the sand from her skirt and hurried across the road.

Anna put her knees up and hugged them to her chest. Such a gorgeous day. It didn't seem right to have the day off, but everyone seemed to be staying well, and Dr. Snow had insisted she rest up for the next emergency that came along. It had been a month since the flu, and she felt he was being too cautious.

Leaning back, she drew a deep breath and thought again about Peter Fielding and the children when a loud bell filled the air. Was it the fire bell? Was there a fire, or, was it something else?

Seconds later Gloria hurried toward her. "Bessie says to come. It's probably a shipwreck and you might be needed."

Anna jumped up, and ran toward the house. A shipwreck. But where? And why so soon? And how could a ship wreck on such a nice day?

Bessie was on the phone. "The shipwreck's down at the bar. You're to go to Dr. Snow's—be ready for whatever."

"I must change—"

"No time for that. Just go, child."

The horse and buggy were brought around and Anna saw Gloria's round face all white and scared looking. She hoped there were no fatalities. Drowning victims were not pleasant to look at.

The fire bell still rang and Anna feared the worst had happened. It was the first continuous one she'd heard since the fire that claimed Rebecca's life.

"A lot of people pray for shipwrecks," Mr. Webster had said one morning at breakfast. "Pray for one so they can get the good things that wash up on shore."

"But if lives are at stake—"

"People don't think about that part."

Bessie had assured her it was true. "Some are out to get all they can get, that's for certain."

"It's a steamer!" Anna heard as she neared town. People ran toward the water as if they could catch sight of the downed vessel, though it was several miles south.

Lizzie stood in the doorway when Anna pulled into the yard.

"I think I'll get used to this feeling of utter helplessness, but one never does. Doctor is on his way. He'll arrive around the same time as the victims."

Anna washed her hands and pinned her cap on. Before she left, Gloria had run down the stairs and out to Anna with it and the cape. At least she partly looked like a nurse.

Dr. Snow arrived minutes later, just as the fire wagon came with two forms in the back. "Put one in the operating room and the other in the examining room."

He told Anna to see to the one being taken to the examining room. She knew later it was because he was alive. The other man was dead. "Died of exposure," Dr. Snow explained. "The poor devil never had a chance." He covered his face with the blanket. "Not much we could do for him, but I think the other fellow has a good chance of making it. Thirty passengers are presumed drowned."

"Thirty!" Anna cried. "How do you know that?"

"It was the *Rosecrans*—a large ship. I don't know how these two got ashore, but ashore they came."

Anna brought the blankets and quilt stored in the closet. With Lizzie's help, they peeled the wet clothes from the sailor's body and bundled him up in thick layers of blankets. "We have to get his temperature up," Anna said. "If we fail, he will die of exposure."

"Not too many survive the ocean's waters," said Lizzie. "I lost a nephew at sea—my sister's boy. Rescued, but it was too late."

"I'm so sorry," Anna murmured, checking the patient's vital signs. It seemed everyone had lost someone at sea. All the old-timers, people who had lived here a long while.

Color began coming back to the cheeks and Anna smiled. "Can you hear me, sir? Do you know where you are?"

The eyes opened and a voice all raspy said, "I've died and gone to heaven and you're an angel."

Anna smiled. "No, sir. You're in Long Beach, Washington. I'm Anna Galloway, a nurse, and you're going to be fine."

Dr. Snow entered the room, examined the man on the bed, looked back at Anna, then at the sailor again. "His color is coming back. Good. Yes, he's going to live to tell about it. Too bad about the others."

It was hours later when the sheriff came to fill them in.

"Another body just floated up on shore."

Anna felt the tightness again. "Another one?"

"Yeah. Already the people are down there, looking for what else that might be washed up on the beach."

Anna remembered Mr. Webster telling about a fellow who lived in Ocean Park finding a case of whiskey while another discovered German beer. Not that Anna thought these such finds, but it amused her.

"Once my grandfather found a beautiful trunk," Lizzie said in the doorway.

"But didn't it belong to someone?"

She shrugged. "In those days they said: 'Finders keepers, losers weepers.' "

Anna shook her head. "I wouldn't want to keep anything that didn't belong to me."

"If you don't take it, it just goes back out to sea and is lost forever."

Still, Anna thought it a strange practice. She wouldn't feel right taking something that belonged to someone else, something that had such a sad tale behind it.

"No more survivors, I fear," Dr. Snow said when the sheriff left. "It was out a far piece—in that bit of water where several have gone down before. Out past the bar, few can survive."

"I think we should pray."

Dr. Snow shook his head. "Pray all you want, Anna, but it will do no good. The Lord giveth and the Lord taketh."

Anna's cheeks burned, as they did when her ire was up. He knew how she believed, yet persisted in saying it did little or no good. Anna went to check on the patient again. She would believe as she wanted. It was much better that way. She poked hairpins back under the heavily starched cap as she hurried down the hall.

ða

Anna was happy to see the shipwreck sailor up and dressed a few days later. Dr. Snow was still out checking on patients, but he had said the man could be released today.

"I suppose you can't wait to get home again," she said, nodding as the man, dressed in new clothes, stood in the doorway of the waiting area. Clothing had been provided by a fund set up for that purpose.

"Aye, missy. The only one who lived to talk about it. Nobody will believe it. Guess I had the luck of the Irish."

Anna wondered what it would be like being the only

survivor—seeing all your friends being swept away, buried at sea.

"I will never forget your kindness to me, your caring. It was your face I first saw and at first I thought I'd gone to meet my Maker."

"Oh, pshaw!" Anna's face flushed. Seeing a nurse under such circumstances gave some patients delusions, and she was used to it. She'd never be pretty, but that didn't matter anymore. Perhaps it had never mattered. She worked with what God had given her.

She watched the door close and the man went to wait for the train that would take him to Megler's Landing. Soon he would be back in Astoria and on another ship heading to the mouth of the Columbia and back across the Pacific Ocean toward home.

The train went by, up through Long Beach. It stopped and she looked out the window as the patient got on. He turned and waved, as if knowing she'd be watching. Others waited to board the train, while others "rubbernecked" as it went by. It was the highlight of the day for many.

Weekends were especially fun during the summer months when the train brought the papas from the city— papas who had not seen their families all week long. Once when Anna had been in Long Beach, she watched one father surrounded by his family. She choked back the tears and felt a wave of homesickness.

She watched until the train disappeared from sight, then went back inside.

# sixteen

A pounding on the front door wakened Wesley Snow. He glanced at the clock beside his bed. Five-thirty in the morning? Small wonder he still felt tired. A frantic voice called out. "Please, Dr. Snow. Come quick!"

He stepped into his pants and grabbed the flannel shirt on the bedpost, throwing it on over his nightshirt.

Peter Fielding stood, holding a still form close. "Doc—it's my Catherine! She's got this red rash—hot as fire! I thought it would go away—but it hasn't."

"Bring her in."

While Peter took Catherine to the back examining room, Wesley scrubbed his hands. He remembered another night when Peter'd brought Callie. O God, was this a repeat?

The child said nothing as Peter laid her on the long table. "Honey, it's going to be okay." Yet even as Peter said the words, his heart almost squeezed shut. He'd told Callie the same thing when she lay so ill, but nothing had saved her. Not prayers, medicine, or his caring for her. He couldn't let Catherine die.

Dr. Snow came and felt the heat emanate from the affected area. He pressed her tummy gently. "Does this hurt, Catherine?"

She shook her head. "No, Dr. Snow."

"Does it hurt here?" He pressed against her inner thigh.

Again, she shook her head.

"She scratches it a lot—says it itches," Peter offered.

Dr. Snow nodded. "That might be how it spread."

*Could it be contagious?* he wondered. *If so, wouldn't Peter and the younger brother have come down with it? Of course it could have a two-week incubation period.* He decided they would treat it as if it were a contagious disease. In the meantime, he would read medical journals to try to find what it was. Oh, for a skin specialist, one who knew about such things. The main thing he must do was stop the raging infection inside that tiny body. If they didn't, she would die. Wesley wondered if Anna might know something about it. She'd been practicing in a large hospital in Cedar Rapids. It certainly wouldn't hurt to ask her when she got in.

Anna arrived an hour later, her cheeks flushed from the chilly morning ride. But she was as mystified as he was. "I have never seen anything like this, Dr. Snow." Her eyes looked from Catherine to Peter, then back at the doctor. "I think we should isolate her, though. At least until we find out what it is."

"That was the conclusion I'd come to."

Dr. Snow looked at Peter's sagging shoulders. "We'll do what we can, Peter. I'll call a colleague in Portland—see what he has to say."

"And I shall attempt to make our patient comfortable," Anna said. She tried to make Catherine laugh as she brought her water and juice—anything in an attempt to flush the disease from the tiny body. She also tried diverting her mind from the problem.

"Once you're through with this rash, we'll have to have another picnic. You'd like that, wouldn't you?"

Catherine nodded, her hand touching Anna's. "I want to get better because Daddy needs me."

*Oh, yes,* Anna thought. *We all need you. Dr. Snow can't let you go.*

When Peter had lost Callie, Wesley had felt responsible. He'd done everything possible, but she had died. His two children were all Peter had in the world. He must save Catherine.

Dr. Snow opened a second medical book. Old and falling apart, it had been a gift from one of his instructors. He looked under rash and there it was. The words leaped out at him. St. Anthony's Fire, so named because of the redness—red as fire—and the heat as in fire—an infection which few recover from. The technical term: *erysipelas.*

He sighed. The new powder that had been discovered in Germany had wonderful powers, but would do no good here. It wasn't the fever they were fighting, it was the infection causing the rash. What could he give her? An open sore, a boil, he could drain. Not so here.

Thoughts of Indian medicine men crossed his mind. Some of the herbs worked. The special medicines had not saved thousands from the measles epidemic, or those afflicted with smallpox, but this was different. He had little faith in herbs and special teas, yet sometimes a doctor was willing to try anything. Peter said he had given the child sassafras tea. Well, it wouldn't do any harm, but it surely hadn't done much good, either.

Wesley drummed a pencil against the medical journal. He needed something to take away the infection, but what? He doubted that anything would work, but somehow he couldn't get Anna's face out of his mind as she spoke earlier of God and miracles and how one must have hope.

Hope. How long since he had thought about hopes, dreams. Desires?

Had Lucinda taken the very life from him when she left? Yet he had felt relief that it was over.

He walked back to the room and inspected the rash again.

"I know what it is now, Anna," he said. "If I just knew how to treat it. What to do."

Anna's eyes lit up. "You *know*?"

He explained the medical term, the common term. "Never have I seen it, but this is what it is. Somehow Catherine got infected—perhaps while playing. He examined her closer. "I see scratches on the inner thigh. I wonder—" He motioned. "Get Peter in here."

"How did she get these scratches?" Dr. Snow asked, pointing to the red marks. "See? They are distinguishable, and it appears to be from rubbing against something. Do you have any idea?"

"She stayed at Doris's—my neighbor's—last week. They—she and Henry played in the barn with the animals. I think—" He paused, nodding. "Yes, I remember Doris saying Catherine had fallen through a hole in the loft. She landed on the hay and though scared, she really wasn't hurt. The hay cushioned her fall."

"That's it!" Wesley Snow stood and began writing frantically on the pad. "I remember the symptoms now. The hay irritated the skin—there are germs in hay—it somehow got into her body through these scratches. She has what we call erysipelas. It's also known as St. Anthony's Fire. Hence the heat, the color. I want you to know—" he met Peter's worried gaze. "I have nothing to

reat this. I don't know if Portland would or not. I can
:all the hospitals there—see if they know how and what
o treat it with. Just knowing is half the battle, Peter."

"Can you save her?"

"I don't—" Dr. Snow stopped, as if thinking twice
»efore speaking. "We're going to try, Peter. We'll certainly
ry."

Peter dozed in the armchair while Anna sponged off
he red area. It was just like fire when she lifted the blan-
:et.

"Anna, about all we can do is keep her comfortable."

Anna stopped sponging the face. "Doctor, I remember a
:ase now. We talked about it in class." Her eyes grew
ound. "That's why it's called St. Anthony's Fire—"

"Did someone named St. Anthony have it?"

"No, but he prayed for those who did. It was early—
around the eleven hundreds—and it was said that those
who believed wholeheartedly were saved by his prayers,
and those who didn't believe, died."

He sighed. "So there is no cure."

"I think a miracle is what we need here."

"Yes, I pray to God you're right."

Anna stopped and stared. *Pray to God?* Was he merely
:aying that, or did he really mean it? If only she knew.

Wesley went out, leaving Anna with the child.

Peter returned that morning, determined to stay until
:he was better.

*And what if we cannot save her?* Wesley had wanted
:o say, but the words that burst from Anna, the look on
aer face as she spoke of God, stopped him. For some
anexplainable reason, he could not get her face out of his
mind. A face that was not beautiful—one that was plain

according to Lucinda—had taken on a radiance that jolted him to his toes. He dismissed the thought and hitched the horses and headed north.

They took turns sitting with Catherine. It reminded Anna of Rebecca, and how she'd prayed for her recovery, all for naught. Anna knew Dr. Snow held out only a slim hope this time, but Anna was confident that Catherine would get well.

It was late when Anna climbed into the buggy and took the reins, praying for the little girl she had grown to love. Catherine was spunky—the apple of her father's eyes. Surely God would hear her fervent prayer. Catherine must be saved.

She stopped the horse and looked into the darkening sky. "God, I've prayed for many things in my life, but never one as needed as this. Please, oh, please save Catherine. Help us to know what to do for her. Amen."

A sudden peace filled Anna as she drove the rest of the way home. It was as if a heavy burden had lifted from her shoulders and she knew, yes, she knew that when she went back in the morning, Catherine would be better. She'd never been more sure of anything in her life.

The rash began to diminish at six o'clock the next morning.

Peter noticed first and jumped up, yelling and crying. "She opened her eyes. My Catherine opened her eyes."

They kept Catherine for two days, making sure she was stabilized. Peter left to go be with Henry when he knew she would be all right. In no time Catherine begged to be let out of bed, asking for her father, her brother.

"You must keep quiet," Anna cautioned her. She brought meals that Lizzie fixed, insisting she stay in bed. But the rash had all but disappeared, and the fire was gone. All that remained were a few scratches, as if reminding them of the illness.

## seventeen

Spring came and with it Anna found golden daffodils, purple hyacinth, and a few weeks later red and yellow tulips bursting through the wet, sandy ground. She clasped her hands in anticipation, wondering what else might be planted in the flower beds around the boarding-house.

She had grown to love the weathered old house with its gables, blue shutters at the windows, and widow's walk on the roof. Someday she might have her own house, but for now this was home. Her home.

One day in March, Peter suggested a drive up the road to the north end. "We never did get past Ocean Park before." His eyes seemed to be teasing her today.

"I'd love to see Oysterville," Anna declared. More oysters were grown there than anywhere else, and shipped to San Francisco on a regular basis. She'd read about how it once was the county seat, but bandits had come across the bay in the middle of the night, stolen the records, and taken them to South Bend. Yes, she wanted to see the end of the peninsula.

The day was warm with a gentle breeze. Anna laughed and waved heartily as they passed others on the plank road. "This is a perfect day for an outing!"

Catherine had rosy cheeks, with little sign she had been at death's door a few months ago. Of course children were resilient, and bounced back after an illness. Anna turned to smile, then laughed when Henry made a face.

"You laugh a lot," Catherine said, fingering the lace on the back of Anna's collar.

Anna turned to stare. "Oh, do I?"

"Yes, you do." Henry added. Now that he knew Anna he'd become quite talkative. Sometimes she referred to him as a chatterbox.

Anna squeezed the small hand. "If you think I laugh a lot, you should hear Albert. He is the jolliest one of the whole family. We call it the Galloway laugh, you know."

"I can attest to that," Peter said with a nod. "But 'tis true. The day *is* brighter when you're along."

The sun was out, birds sang from the trees as the horses trotted down the road. Peter drove the team of workhorses today since they were going so far. "This long trip is too much for ole Gopher," he had explained earlier.

Anna began singing songs she'd learned from Sarah, and soon they all joined in. "Yankee Doodle went to town, riding on a pony. Stuck a feather in his hat and called it Macaroni."

Anna leaned over and stuck a feather in the brim of Catherine's straw hat. She shrieked with delight, then stuck it in her father's hatband.

"I like 'O Susanna,' Peter said. "Do you remember it, Anna?"

"Of course I do. It's the craziest song Stephen Foster ever wrote."

"Why, Anna?" Catherine asked.

Anna laughed. "Just listen to the lyrics and tell me what you think."

"O I' goin' to Alabamy for my true love for to see, it rained so hot the day I left, the weather it was dry.

O Susanna, don't you cry for me, for I'm going' to Alabamy with my banjo on my knee."

"That's funny!" Catherine said. "How can it rain if the weather is dry?"

"That's exactly what I mean."

They sang on, including "Polly Wolly Doodle All the Day" and "Dixie."

"We may not be southern, but we need to learn the old songs," Anna claimed.

Once the wind swept up, and Anna's hand instinctively reached up to hold her hat. It was a pink straw with a wide brim, another Bessie'd found in her closet, but it had ties under the chin and was perfect for a drive.

Peter chuckled, but looked straight ahead. "Thought I was going to have to rescue your hat, did you?"

Anna laughed again. She loved the view of the ocean with its magnificent waves, the trees, and brush alongside the road. Occasionally they would see a road and a house in the distance. She doubted she'd ever tire of its beauty.

"I'm thinking about taking on a new job," Peter said, breaking the silence.

"A new job? You won't be logging anymore?"

A frown creased his forehead. "I'll be working the cranberry bogs—a bit closer to home. The children need me, though my neighbor takes good care of them."

"Are you sure about this, Peter? I thought you liked logging."

"I'll still do that, just not as much."

"I see."

"You do like it here, don't you, Anna?" Peter said then.

"Yes," Anna replied. Somehow she could not imagine

ever leaving here to go anywhere else.

Peter's gaze was intense. "It's just like I told you that first day when we were coming on the train."

"And you were right."

Peter let the reins go slack, then pulled over, though it wasn't necessary. Nobody was behind them on the nearly deserted stretch of road. "Would you ever consider giving up nursing?"

"Give up nursing?" Anna couldn't believe Peter could even ask the question. "No. I like my work. Why do you ask?"

He shrugged. "A nurse is dedicated to her job, right? This means you will never marry or become a mother."

Anna's heart nearly stopped. "But, Peter, nursing is what I know. There's such a need here."

His face was somber. Anna swallowed. She should have realized why Peter stopped by the boardinghouse so often these days. She felt little arms wrap around her neck, and though no words were spoken, she knew Catherine had heard.

Peter picked up the reins again. "We're almost there." The sun had gone behind a cloud, making the sky darken. Anna felt a sudden chill as the buildings of the town loomed into sight with the beautiful Shoalwater Bay to the east. It seemed she was replaying another scene from the past, as she thought of Joseph who had expected her to give up her career.

They stopped and sat along the bay, eating sandwiches and drinking lemonade. Catherine and Henry ran off to play on the sandy beach. Anna relaxed as she watched them. No worries had they. She leaned back, surveying the beauty before her. She could not imagine never marrying or having children, but perhaps that's what God would have her do.

Peter wasn't about to let the subject drop. "Suppose someone needed you terribly bad? Suppose there were children who needed a mother to care for them?"

Anna felt a smile tug at the corners of her mouth. "I don't suppose their names are Catherine and Henry?"

"And what if they are?" Peter leaned over and wrote her name in the sand. "Anna, surely you must know I get lonely. I'm not good with words—"

Anna wasn't good with words either. At least not now. Peter needed her, but what of her needs? Did they matter at all?

"You look distressed."

"I do?"

"Perhaps this isn't the right time. Perhaps I should wait. I know how upset you are about the little girl who died—"

"Peter, I—" She turned away. She could not say the words that were in her mind and heart. She just couldn't. If he didn't understand now, how could she expect him to understand later? She wanted to be needed. Wasn't that why she had gone into nursing? But she also wanted to be loved. Love was important if one took that final step into marriage. Both had to love with their whole hearts. How could she expect anything less to work? Lucinda had not loved Wesley Snow. She didn't care about him at all. Anna loved Peter like a brother. She realized that now as she looked at him with the sun hitting his sandy hair. A marriage of convenience was not right, nor was it for her.

Catherine ran up and dumped a handful of small bits of driftwood at Anna's feet. "Just for you, Anna." Her small face beamed.

"And I found some, too," Henry added to the pile.

"Oh, you two are so wonderful to think of me that way." She hugged each of them, then looked back at Peter who seemed to be deep in thought. Of course he didn't understand, just as she didn't fully. One thing Anna knew was that Peter still loved his wife, or the memory of her. It was apparent when he said her name, the way he talked about her, the way he had not let himself open his heart to anyone. She supposed he had to her a bit, but not as he should. One must open his heart all the way. That was Anna's dream. Anna's hope. Some day there might be someone who would offer all of his heart, no strings attached.

The fog rolled in, and Anna gathered the wood, sticking it in the pockets of her coat, her dress, and the rest into the apron she often wore to the beach.

"We better head back." Peter grabbed the blanket and shook the sand out. They folded it together, neither saying anything. Peter helped her into the front of the wagon, while the children clamored into the back.

"It was just a thought, Anna. Just a thought," he said once they were on the way.

The children seemed oblivious to their conversation, oblivious to the fact that their father had just asked Anna to be their mother. If they had known, they would have urged her to say yes, assuring her they loved her, for she knew they did, just as she loved them. But one must have more than that. She couldn't help but believe that to be true.

"It's going to be very late when we get back," Peter said.

Soon Catherine and Henry fell asleep and Anna was

deep in her thoughts. A proposal. Mama would have said, "Yes, Anna, marry. Have children. You'll be a good mother. A good wife." She was certain Pearl and Emily would agree. And Bessie. Bessie who had loved her captain would probably say Anna needed someone. Yet Bessie might not agree. It was something to talk over with her. She'd know what Anna should do.

When they arrived at Seaview, Peter turned and took Anna's hand. "Thank you for going with us, for making our day special." He helped her down.

"It was a wonderful day—a wonderful trip," she answered softly.

Stars twinkled from above as she stood under the canopy of tree branches, praying to God she would say the proper thing, make the right decision.

"Peter, I'm fond of you, and the children. It's just that—"

"Sh-h—say no more. Sleep on it." He bent down and brushed his lips across her cheek. "I'll see you in a few days."

*Do you love me, Peter Fielding?* Anna wanted to ask as she watched his retreating back and listened as the buggy drove out of sight.

It was late, and everyone had gone to bed, even Bessie. As Anna tiptoed up the steps, she thought of Peter from that first meeting on the *T.J. Potter*. He had been kind enough to help. He had taken her clamming, on picnics, on Sunday drives after church. Always courteous and polite. *But, does he love me?* she wondered again.

After her Bible reading and her evening prayer, Anna looked out at the dark sky. It was going to rain. She could always tell now. It didn't matter though, as the day had been flawlessly perfect for the drive.

The rain started up slowly, building to a roaring windstorm, and Anna snuggled under the heavy quilts, burying all but her eyes and the tip of her nose. The rat-a-tat on the roof calmed her somehow, made her glad she was inside where it was warm and cozy.

The storm matched the turmoil in her mind, her pounding heart. "Leave it to You, God, to send me a storm to quell my anxious thoughts."

# eighteen

Monday morning came, and with it a renewal to continue with her nursing. Anna wanted to see Peter and the children again. She enjoyed them so much. Couldn't they go on as before?

Dressing quickly, she brushed her hair, which was growing out in all directions. It was especially contrary after a night of sleeping on it. She stuck in extra hairpins, as the cap wouldn't be able to make it stay down. Anna made her bed and headed down the stairs for breakfast. A smell of bread baking filled her with sudden hunger.

Anna nodded at Mr. Webster, Miss Fern, who had returned from an extended vacation, and Cora, who would be leaving soon. She'd decided to move back to New York where her parents owned a farm.

Bessie came with a platter of sliced ham, biscuits, and gravy. She asked the blessing, then hurried back to the kitchen for the coffee.

"And so, how was the trip up north?" she asked.

Anna glowed at the memory of the day. "It's more primitive at that end, though I enjoyed seeing Nahcotta. Peter pointed out where the train stops and turns around. And the bay! The water was as smooth as glass, nothing like the ocean side."

Bessie nodded. " 'Tis a different beauty up that way. Come. Let's sit in the parlor a minute before ye leave for work. I know something is troubling ye."

"You do?" Anna looked at the mantel clock. "I only have a few minutes."

"I know. I'll get to the point."

Anna felt uneasy without knowing why.

"Did Peter ask ye anything?"

She set her cup into the saucer hastily, sloshing coffee out.

"Peter talked to you?" She couldn't believe she'd be the last to know.

"Indeed not. Does ye think I'm everyone's mother?"

"But, how did you—"

"Know?" She finished Anna's question. "Child, I've lived long enough to know when people are happy, and when they are not. Peter has not been happy since Callie died. Only recently has there been a gleam in his eyes, a lighter step as he walks."

A knife seemed to twist inside Anna. "Oh, Bessie, I don't know if I can say yes to his proposal, though I am quite fond of him."

"It's the doctor, isn't it?"

Anna's heart quickened. "Why would you think Dr. Snow has anything to do with it?"

"I've been watching ye. Watching him. Noticing the way his voice changes when ye walk into the room."

"Oh, Bessie, no! Never. He loves Lucinda. I know he does. This has bothered him considerably—that they argued and she left on an angry note."

"Then why didn't he go after her?"

"Because his work is here. This is his life. These people." *Just as it is mine,* she suddenly thought.

"Lucinda is beautiful. He could never love me in that way. Never." She knew her reasoning to be sound. "If there is any admiration from Wesley Snow, it has to do with my ability as a nurse."

Bessie just smiled. "His admiration goes much deeper than that, Anna. Trust me to know what I'm a-seeing."

Anna rose to leave, but Bessie's words rang through her mind as the horse clip-clopped down the street toward Long Beach.

Wesley Snow had already left when Anna arrived. Lizzie looked up from a pile of sand she was sweeping into a dustpan. "Doctor says he won't be back in time for lunch today—for you to go on and leave if nobody comes in."

"I can wait until he returns."

"Said he'd be gone all day. Oysterville's a fair piece, you know."

Anna removed her cap. "I now know how far it is, Lizzie. Peter drove me and the children up there yesterday. What they need is a physician for that end of the peninsula."

Lizzie shook her head. "Doubt one would come so far. It took a long time to find Dr. Snow. Most doctors prefer the cities."

Anna walked down the hall to the recovery room. As she straightened the room, she thought of Rebecca. It had been weeks since she had been here, and subsequently died of her burns.

It was as if Anna could still see the small form, smell the stench of burning flesh, and was wishing and praying she could relieve the child's pain. She now prayed she'd never see another person suffer as Rebecca had. She often prayed for the father who had come home from logging to find not only his wife and older child dead from the fire, but to learn he had also lost his youngest the next day.

Anna checked the cabinet and noticed they were low on petroleum jelly and bandages.

"Do you know if Dr. Snow placed an order for supplies yet?"

"No, he didn't," Lizzie replied. "He mentioned it just this morning before leaving. Why don't you go ahead and send it?"

The supplies were sent from Portland, coming to the peninsula in the same way Anna had. Up the boat, across the Columbia, and then on the railroad. Anna could at least save him that task, as he'd be exhausted by the time he returned.

The day seemed endless. Not only did Anna not have patients to tend to, she had nothing else to do. The files were in order, supplies ordered, Lizzie had finished the cleaning and had gone to her room for an afternoon nap. Anna had straightened the furniture in the living room for the fifth time when she realized what was wrong. She hadn't seen Wesley Snow that morning, nor had she seen him yesterday. She missed him. She wanted to see him, wanted to make him smile, longed to reach up and touch the lock of hair that fell across his forehead. Wanted to tell him that she cared, though she knew she shouldn't.

It was Bessie's doings—she'd put the idea in Anna's head, filling her with notions about Dr. Snow. She shook her head. No, it couldn't be true. Bessie did not know everything, though she often professed to. How could she be in a quandary about this? It was Peter she should be thinking about. Peter who wanted her decision. Peter and the children who needed her.

She decided to write to Pearl. Maybe Pearl could shed light on the questions that tormented her heart so. She found paper and pen in the desk.

> *Dearest Sister, Pearl,*
> *How are you and the expected baby doing?*
> *Fine, I trust.*

Anna chewed on the pen's nib. Now to go on with her question, but how was she to start?

> *I am writing for advice. Yes, me, your eldest*
> *sister, asking the youngest member of the family.*
> *How did you know when you loved Paul? Did it*
> *come on gradual-like, or was it suddenly there? I*
> *thought I loved Joseph and perhaps I did, in a way,*
> *but my feelings are much stronger for a certain*
> *person who will go unnamed. I do not want to*
> *make a fool of myself. I could not bear to do that.*
> *I implore you to write to me as quickly as possible*
> *and to please write personal on the outside of the*
> *envelope.*

Anna paused for a moment. Her mail came to the boardinghouse, but she did not want the answer to go there. She would ask Pearl to send it General Delivery in care of Long Beach. Perhaps Tioga Station would be good. Or the Breakers Hotel.

She addressed the envelope and put it into the pocket of her uniform to mail later that afternoon.

Pacing back and forth, Anna wondered what she would tell Peter. He needed her answer, needed to get his life back in order.

When Lizzie rose from her nap, Anna excused herself, saddled the horse and drove north to Tioga Station. The letter would go out today. She could conceivably receive an answer by next Monday.

She paused at the door of the post office, wondering if she should mail the letter. What might Pearl think about her older sister?

She bought a two-cent stamp and handed the letter over the counter.

"Aren't you Miss Galloway, our nurse?" the woman asked.

Anna smiled. "Yes, I work for Dr. Snow."

"I'm happy you are here. Dr. Snow is much too busy for one man. It's nice that someone can relieve him." He smiled. "I heard about the little feller in the candy store. And it was my cousin who had the fishhook in his foot."

Anna laughed. "Every one seems to be related in some way here. I must be careful and not say anything for fear of offending a relative." It was the postmaster's turn to laugh now. "You are so right. I wasn't born here, but many were. Many will also die here."

Anna headed back. Her thoughts about Dr. Snow were ludicrous. He needed her far more as a nurse than as a possible wife. What could she possibly be thinking of? She had the sudden urge to run back in and ask for her letter back. What would Pearl think? And Emily? That she had gone daft? Nurses fell in love with doctors all the time, just as some students fall in love with their teachers. It was admiration, that was all.

How could she ever leave nursing? Her heart pounded when she saw the familiar wagon pulled up at the side. What was wrong? Had he changed his mind about going north? She stayed outside for a long moment and drew in deep breaths. She *did* love the doctor. Even so, it was something she'd keep buried deep inside her. Only she and God would know.

# nineteen

Wesley Snow leaned over and turned off the lamp. It had been another long day. A momentous week. Spring had come and with it came more accidents. Fewer fires, thank goodness, but definitely more accidents. He'd felt such relief when little Catherine Fielding had pulled through. He'd seen her on Sunday, and she was as pretty and robust as ever. She and Anna were a pair. Anna must have been that kind of child, for she was certainly that sort of woman. Full of vigor, laughter, always seeing the best. That's what he needed; someone to remind him of bright side of the life. If one dwelled on the good things, the negative was much dimmer.

Anna. That smile. The eyes so intense, yet loving and caring. Her crazy, wild hair with a mind of its own. How fitting. Just yesterday, he had longed to reach out and touch her.

Why had he thought of that now, just before bedtime? Now when sleep should come, giving him the much-needed rest? And then Wesley Snow recognized there were times when he felt lonely. Bereft. He knew without wondering twice what Anna would say about that. And then it came to him. Swiftly and surely. He had not seen Anna Galloway today and he knew how much he had missed seeing her. Missed the smile, the laugh that came from deep within.

He pulled back the quilt and slipped under the cold covers. He hadn't much time to think about it before, not even when he was betrothed to Lucinda, but it might be nice to snuggle up to someone, to share her warmth.

Wesley punched his pillow. What was wrong with him? At thirty he should be content in his position. Perhaps someone would come along one day, but for now he would concentrate on doctoring. He had things to do, people to help. He needed a wife, but not just yet.

It was an hour before Wesley found the needed rest, and then only after praying. Seeking forgiveness for straying, for those years of turning his back on God, for rejecting the faith his mother had instilled in him. He'd been bitter when his mother died, railing at everyone. This bitterness made him turn to study. And though he found solace in practicing medicine, there were times when his inner soul cried out for something more.

Wesley prayed, for the first time in a very long time, for God to help him, to guide his steps.

☙

Anna could not sleep that night. Exhausted from a twelve-hour schedule, sleep evaded her, as her mind whirled with a hundred scattering thoughts. She'd read the 139th Psalm twice. There was meaning for her there. She just had to find it.

*O Lord, thou hast searched me and known me. . .*

She knew that to be true.

*If I take the wings of the morning and dwell in the uttermost parts of the sea*
*Even there shall thy hand lead me, and thy right hand shall hold me.*

Tears slipped from her eyes as Anna remembered that day in the ocean, the waves tossing her about as if she'd been a toothpick. God had been there. Her life had been spared.

She closed her Bible and asked for God's leading in the troubles of the moment. *God, I don't know when I first started loving Dr. Snow. Please take my thoughts away and help me to love Peter who needs me. If it is Thy will.*

Anna wondered when she had first started loving Dr. Snow. It had crept up on her like a measles rash, only much, much slower.

Working with him, at his side, day in and day out, she noticed a gentleness, a fierce determination to be a good doctor. He lived to serve others. Anna had known dedicated doctors in Iowa, but Dr. Snow was different somehow.

Anna had realized long ago that knowing him at a deeper level would never materialize. She would admire and love him day in and day out, but it ended there. The thought that he might find her attractive never occurred to her. How could she possibly ever compete with the charming Lucinda Lawson? Then there was his manner. It was so often brusque and impatient, Anna had given up trying to please.

*Did you ever stop to think that brusqueness is a cover-up?*

Anna's heart pounded. Could that be? Why had it not occurred to her before?

But there was Lucinda, and she had not given up. She'd returned to the peninsula again in April, just as the rhododendrons were in full bloom. Anna had never seen such beauty, but beauty was wasted on Lucinda. She had a mission, and that was to win Dr. Snow back. She also had a vendetta against Anna, and Anna did her best to avoid her.

Lucinda was not one to discourage easily. "I want you, Wesley Snow, and I aim to get you one way or the other!" Her blond curls looked like fat sausages framing her pale face. The dark green taffeta dress swirled around her slender hips as she flounced from the building.

She left a week later, to everyone's relief. Still Anna wondered if Wesley was really over her.

The day after Anna's sleepless night Wesley found her in the supply room, checking over the clean linens. "Are you hiding in here?" A smile lit up his broad face.

"Who, me?" She stifled a giggle.

"I want to stay here. Help these people. Portland has plenty of doctors. I'm needed here. Don't you agree, Anna?" He took the stack of towels and placed them back on the shelf. His blue eyes, with their warm gaze, reminded her of cornflowers that grew wild in the field close to home. They watched her now with an intenseness that baffled her.

She met his gaze and felt the color creep to her skin. Perhaps he was waiting for her to answer his question. "You are needed here, yes."

"I've done some thinking. Last night when I couldn't sleep. And you are needed also, Anna. You're good with the patients. They trust you. When I make my calls, someone always asks how my short-haired nurse is."

Anna laughed then. It had come from her depths, practically shaking the windows. She covered her mouth immediately.

Dr. Snow looked serious. "Don't hide your laugh, Anna Galloway. It's a wonderful, warm laugh. It cheers me up."

Anna looked down. He moved closer, his hands lifting her chin. She felt his warm breath on her neck. She fought back the impulse to touch his face, to bring it even closer. His gaze lingered.

"Anna, I need you," he said, breaking the silence.

"I don't think you know what you're saying," she finally said. She couldn't have heard right. This couldn't be. He loved Lucinda. She knew he did. It was a game of cat and mouse they'd been playing to see who was the most stubborn. She'd heard about the white satin wedding dress with its layers of tulle.

"Anna, must I say more?"

How could she respond? Her need was great, but others' needs superseded hers. Patients needed her. The peninsula needed her. Peter's motherless children needed her. Her family needed her.

But what of love? She wanted someone to love her. Need was necessary, but love was also important. How could she build a life on anything less? Then there was his lack of faith, the most important reason of all.

"Anna?" Wesley Snow's voice was close, too close. "Say something. When you are quiet, I know you're mulling things over."

Anna pressed her hands to her side. Yes, Dr. Snow would know that about her. Hadn't they worked side by side for the past nine months? He observed his patients, just as he watched and understood his nurse. She would have been surprised if he had done any less.

She turned and raised her face to his. "I think your need is to continue being a doctor, whether it's here or in Portland. And Lucinda waits."

"That's over. She does not want to live here and I do

not want to live there. It's been settled."

Anna looked out at the empty waiting room. No one was there, but at any moment an emergency could arise. And if so, she would answer the call. "I have a calling, too, and it's just as great as yours. Women are not thought of as equal and I hope that may change someday."

"Anna, Anna, I have never thought of you as any less just because you're a woman."

"If not, you are one of the few."

"I believe God has created all men to be equal, and I use that term *men* in a general sense."

Anna's heart pounded. *God created? Had he really said that?*

She met his gaze. "I think you are lonely and I don't want to be someone who merely fills the void in your life, Dr. Snow—"

"Wesley."

"Wesley."

"Lucinda is incapable of loving anyone but herself. I learned after our engagement that she must marry before she could receive her grandfather's inheritance. I believe she has found someone who can fulfill that role."

"She was marrying you to inherit money?"

"Yes."

Anna walked to the other end of the room. She must keep busy. Perhaps get a cup of coffee. She straightened the doilies on the tables and stacked the few books. The waiting room always got so messy.

"I'm going to ask Lizzie to fix us something to eat." Dr. Snow turned and left the room. As darkness encroached, from a storm brewing, Anna's mind whirled with a hundred thoughts.

The sound of thundering hooves filled the air. The door flew open and a young man cried, "Oh, thank, God, someone is here! I need help and quick!"

Dr. Snow and Anna ran out into the darkness. A hay wagon was pulled up to the door and inside a man lay writhing in pain. Anna bent down to investigate, then stopped. Peter Fielding lay in the wagon, blood coursing down his right leg. "Peter!" she gasped.

Wesley summed up the situation and ordered him brought into the examining room. Minutes later, the pants leg was cut off and a tourniquet was applied to the limb.

"My God, man, how did this happen?"

Peter's face was ashen, his eyes rolled in the back of his head.

"Clearing property. Wind turned and the tree came the wrong way. Tried to get out of the way—but it got his leg," the driver said.

Anna came with blankets. Peter was in shock, and the next few minutes were crucial. "It's going to be all right," she said, sponging his face gently. "You're going to be okay. Dr. Snow will see to that."

"My kids," he moaned, "I can't die and leave my kids."

Anna choked back sudden tears. "Peter, I'm praying for His mercy." She took his hand and prayed aloud, prayed for healing and that God would comfort him.

"Anna," Dr. Snow called. "I need your help here."

The blood had stopped gushing, but the cut was deep. Nasty. "Get the antiseptic. The large needle, then I'll need you to hold this while I stitch."

It seemed to take forever as Anna watched and Dr. Snow sutured the gaping wound. He had administered morphine and Peter was no longer in pain.

"He's going to make it. Another ten minutes and I wouldn't have been as positive."

Anna reached over, wiping the perspiration from his brow. "I knew it to be so."

"It's him you love, isn't it?"

Anna's heart thudded again. Peter? Did she love Peter? No. She had thought so once, but realized she loved him as a brother, would always love him as a brother. She trembled as her thoughts turned to Dr. Snow. They had much in common. Their love for and interest in medicine. In helping others. The love of this primitive area that time had all but forgotten. And he had mentioned God tonight in a loving manner.

More horses hooves filled the night air and Anna stared at Wesley. "Not another emergency!"

The door opened, bringing the coldness of the advancing wind, and a woman appeared in the doorway, screaming, "They told me he was hurt, and I feared, oh, how I feared the doctor wouldn't be in!" She gasped when she saw Peter's face. "Oh, no, Peter! Peter please hear me!"

Dr. Snow put a hand on the woman's shoulder. "Mrs. Yates, he's going to make it. You must settle down; it won't do him any good to see you like this."

*Of course,* Anna thought, looking at the distraught face, wisps of hair pulled loose from the knot at the nape. Peter's neighbor, Doris. They had never met, but Anna'd heard a lot about her.

Doris stepped back, her eyes never leaving Peter's still form. "I take care of Catherine and Henry. They play with my own three kids—they're like family. And Peter—" her voice choked, "Peter is—oh—"

But her eyes said it all, Anna realized, as the woman

bent over him again. She loved him. This was need, yes, but it was love, and perhaps Doris had not known it until now. The fear of losing him had brought it to the surface.

Anna washed her hands, the sobs she'd held back so long finally releasing. She felt a hand on her shoulder, and took a deep breath.

"Anna, it's okay to cry. Why do you think God made tears?"

"I—I—" she turned and met Wesley's piercing gaze.

"There's no need to say anything." His hand brushed back a curl that had escaped from under the cap. "I guess I knew all along how you felt about Peter."

His words whirled inside her mind, as she realized what he thought. Of course he thought she loved Peter, that if she were to marry anyone it would be him.

Dr. Snow left the room to check on the patient. Peter's eyes were opening and Doris sat holding his hand, speaking to him in a low voice. "Doc says you're going to be fine as frog's hair—just need a few weeks to recuperate." She smiled through the tears. "And I'll be here a-waiting. You can count on that."

Dr. Snow wondered about love and need and how mixed up things could be. Clearly this woman loved Peter with her whole heart, while Anna loved Peter and he loved Anna. The thought of losing Anna filled him with anguish. He could see that same fear mirrored on Doris's face. She'd lost one husband and did not want to lose the man she now loved. Why were there always complications?

Anna sterilized the instruments and washed the towels while she thought of Peter, his last words to her about getting married, giving Catherine and Henry a home. How she had not answered him, and felt guilt for rebuff-

ng him. She wondered now if he had been a mite care-
ess and cut the tree wrong. She'd heard tell it could hap-
en. Footsteps approached. Dr. Snow shook his head. "It
vas too close, Anna. Way too close."

"You are wrong about Peter," she said then.

"Wrong?"

Anna turned and looked into his eyes. She knew she
vould never tire of looking at the kindness, the concern,
he way his eyes mesmerized her, the jutting chin, the
lean-shaven face. She wanted to touch him—longed to
ouch him.

"I refused Peter's proposal last Sunday."

"You did?"

Anna nodded. "He—you see—we would never be able
o agree on certain things and I think of him as a good
riend. I don't want to lose him as a friend—not ever—
ut I cannot marry a friend."

"Anna—" He came closer, his mouth against her hair.
"If Peter isn't in line, let me be the first one there."

She didn't move—couldn't move. "There is no line."

"If there isn't, there should be."

She slipped into his embrace, asking God if it had been
His plan all along—if that was why she had come to this
lace.

"I need you, Anna, it is true, but far more important I
ove you with my whole heart. If you think you could
ver feel anything for me. . ."

Anna met his gaze again and her eyes answered his
question. "How about till death do us part?" she whis-
ered, her head leaning against his thick chest.

The front door blew open as another gust of wind hit
he small North Beach Peninsula, but neither the doctor

or nurse noticed as they stood side by side as they had stood many times in the past. This time—as soon as arrangements could be made—it would be as man and wife.

# A Letter To Our Readers

Dear Reader:

In order that we might better contribute to your reading enjoyment, we would appreciate your taking a few minutes to respond to the following questions. When completed, please return to the following:

Rebecca Germany, Managing Editor
Heartsong Presents
P.O. Box 719
Uhrichsville, Ohio 44683

1. Did you enjoy reading *Anna's Hope?*
   ❑ Very much. I would like to see more books by this author!
   ❑ Moderately
   I would have enjoyed it more if _____

   _____

2. Are you a member of **Heartsong Presents**? ❑Yes ❑No
   If no, where did you purchase this book?_____

   _____

3. What influenced your decision to purchase this book? (Check those that apply.)

   ❑ Cover          ❑ Back cover copy

   ❑ Title          ❑ Friends

   ❑ Publicity      ❑ Other_____

4. How would you rate, on a scale from 1 (poor) to 5 (superior), the cover design?_____

5. On a scale from 1 (poor) to 10 (superior), please rate
   the following elements.

   ___Heroine        ___Plot

   ___Hero           ___Inspirational theme

   ___Setting        ___Secondary characters

6. What settings would you like to see covered in
   **Heartsong Presents** books?_____

   _____

   _____

7. What are some inspirational themes you would like
   to see treated in future books?_____

   _____

   _____

8. Would you be interested in reading other **Heartsong
   Presents** titles?        ❑ Yes        ❑ No

9. Please check your age range:
   ❑ Under 18        ❑ 18-24        ❑ 25-34
   ❑ 35-45           ❑ 46-55        ❑ Over 55

10. How many hours per week do you read? _____

Name _____

Occupation_____

Address_____

City_____ State_____ Zip _____

# An Old-Fashioned Christmas

*Four new inspirational love stories
from Christmases gone by*

**God Jul by Tracie Peterson**

Sigrid may be resigned to spinsterhood, but she is not ready to sell the family homestead. Two men have approached her about marriage. In whose ear will Sigrid whisper "God Jul" (Merry Christmas)?

**Chrsitmas Flower by Colleen L. Reece**

Thana cannot ignore the feeling that God is leading her away from her beloved Alaska. But what about her childhood friend, Wyatt, who insists on following her all the way to North Carolina?

**For the Love of a Child by Sally Laity**

This Christmas, can two lonely adults be drawn togher by the plaintive cry of a child in the cold Philadelphia night?

**Miracle on Kismet Hill by Loree Lough**

High on Kismet Hill, Brynne surveys the magnificent vista below and wonders about her future, ravaged by the Civil War. One man she loved could be dead, one man she loved betrayed her, and the third. . . She simply can't risk being wrong again.

(352 pages, Paperbound, 5" x 8")

# ······Hearts♥ng ······

## HEARTSONG PRESENTS TITLES AVAILABLE NOW:

(If ordering from this page, please remember to include it with the order form.)

# ········ Presents ········

### Great Inspirational Romance at a Great Price!

**Heartsong Presents** books are inspirational romances in contemporary and historical settings, designed to give you an enjoyable, spirit-lifting reading experience. You can choose wonderfully written titles from some of today's best authors like Peggy Darty, Sally Laity, Tracie Peterson, Colleen L. Reece, Lauraine Snelling, and many others.

*When ordering quantities less than twelve, above titles are $2.95 each.*
*Not all titles may be available at time of order.*

# Hearts♥ng Presents
## *Love Stories Are Rated G!*

That's for godly, gratifying, and of course, great! If you lov
a thrilling love story, but don't appreciate the sordidness of son
popular paperback romances, **Heartsong Presents** is for you. I
fact, **Heartsong Presents** is the *only inspirational romance boc
club*, the only one featuring love stories where Christian faith
the primary ingredient in a marriage relationship.

Sign up today to receive your first set of four, never befor
published Christian romances. Send no money now; you wi
receive a bill with the first shipment. You may cancel at any tin
without obligation, and if you aren't completely satisfied wit
any selection, you may return the books for an immediate refund

Imagine. . .four new romances every four weeks—two histor
cal, two contemporary—with men and women like you who lon
to meet the one God has chosen as the love of their lives. . .all fe
the low price of $9.97 postpaid.

*To join, simply complete the coupon below and mail to th*
*address provided.* **Heartsong Presents** romances are rated G fe
another reason: They'll arrive *Godspeed!*

---

# YES! Sign me up for Hearts♥ng!

**NEW MEMBERSHIPS WILL BE SHIPPED IMMEDIATELY!**
**Send no money now.** We'll bill you only $9.97 post-paid with your first
shipment of four books. Or for faster action, call toll free 1-800-847-8270.

NAME _____

ADDRESS _____

CITY _____ STATE _____ ZIP _____

**MAIL TO:** HEARTSONG PRESENTS, P.O. Box 719, Uhrichsville, Ohio 44683

YES10-9(